NO LEGACY FOR LINDSAY

Lindsay Macrae crossed the world with her young stepbrother and stepsister to give them a home. They arrived in New Zealand too late to know their father, but their future, Lindsay learned, was entrusted to his farm manager, Euan Hazeldean, who soon made it very clear that Lindsay was not welcome.

Love is
a time of enchantment:
in it all days are fair and all fields
green. Youth is blest by it,
old age made benign:
the eyes of love see
roses blooming in December,
and sunshine through rain. Verily
is the time of true-love
a time of enchantment — and
Oh! how eager is woman
to be bewitched!

ESSIE SUMMERS

NO LEGACY
FOR LINDSAY

Complete and Unabridged

ULVERSCROFT
Leicester

First published in Great Britain in 1965 by
Mills & Boon Limited
London

First Large Print Edition
published November 1993
by arrangement with
Mills & Boon Limited
London

British Library CIP Data

Summers, Essie
    No legacy for Lindsay.—Large print ed.—
Ulverscroft large print series: romance
I. Title
823 [F]

ISBN 0–7089–2976–1

Published by
F. A. Thorpe (Publishing) Ltd.
Anstey, Leicestershire

Set by Words & Graphics Ltd.
Anstey, Leicestershire
Printed and bound in Great Britain by
T. J. Press (Padstow) Ltd., Padstow, Cornwall

This book is printed on acid-free paper

1

LINDSAY MACRAE stared incredulously at Mrs. Lockhart. She shook her head a little as if to clear her hearing.

"I can't have heard you right, surely," she said. "You aren't really suggesting that I should put Callum and Morag in a home?"

Mrs. Lockhart gave a tiny sigh that was meant to indicate she was being most patient and reasonable. "My dear, you are so young . . . When we are a little older we learn to accept these things and realize life isn't always ideal . . . That we sometimes have to put up with second best. It will be kinder to the children in the long run."

"I'm not concerned with long run," said Lindsay fiercely. "I'm concerned with *now*. They may be orphans, but they have me — their sister!"

"Their half sister."

"Well, their half sister. What difference

does that make? I love them just as much as if their father had been my father."

"That's where it could be difficult . . . later. How are you to know how they'll turn out? An irresponsible man for their father, one who deserted their mother when she needed him most!"

Lindsay bit her lip. It was so true.

"But that doesn't matter. There are rogues in everyone's ancestry, I suppose. Neither of the children shows any signs of taking after him. And they were brought up by my mother — brought up well. They never even saw their father."

"Children are not always the better for being brought up by only a woman. Your mother spoiled those children."

Lindsay's cheeks showed a fleck of color, but she spoke quietly and with conviction. "She didn't, you know. Just because her ideas on the way to bring up children and your ideas differed is not to say hers were wrong."

Mrs. Lockhart's lips tightened. "That's impertinence!"

Lindsay drew herself a little taut to control her trembling. This was horrible — quarreling with Robin's mother.

2

Something she had avoided till now. "It wasn't meant to be impertinent. But I cannot allow you to say my mother spoiled the twins. She simply had very little trouble with them. They're strong willed but biddable. As a teacher, mother knew children so well, and ruled by love."

Lindsay's heart quailed as she saw the expression in the black eyes in front of her. What was wrong with that?

"More impertinence! Just because Alastair left home it's not to say it was my fault . . . that I failed as a mother, that I was too hard on him."

Lindsay made a distressed movement with her hands. "Oh, please! I didn't mean that. You didn't have trouble with Alastair, really. It was simply that he wanted to be independent. Lots of young men want their own homes when they're married. Alastair was offered that job as a married shepherd living in one of the cottages, and took it. Anyway, I wasn't even thinking of Alastair."

"Were you not? I always thought you put him up to going off like that. Imagine — he could have been running this farm

3

with Robin, his own master. Instead of that he's nothing but a hired hand."

Lindsay said hesitatingly, "But — but he seems very happy, and he and Nessie are saving like mad against the day they'll own their own place. But in any case, it's nothing to do with me — it never was — and this situation is rather different, isn't it?" She attempted a laugh. "After all, you've bought that place in town near your sister. That was your own idea, so the children won't annoy you. I agree it would have been difficult for you otherwise. It's not easy for an older woman to take young children into her home. But there's plenty of room here for my little brother and sister."

"You agreed with Alastair that a couple should start off on their own . . . aren't you hoist with your own petard now? No couple should start off with a ready-made family. You and Robin would be better alone."

"It's quite different in the case of young children. It's never easy living in a home with one's mother-in-law . . . and far from easy for the mother-in-law either, to be fair; it must be

4

very hard to relinquish the reins. You're not suggesting I desert the children, are you? They've never known a father, they've not long lost their mother. How could I?"

"It wouldn't be a matter of deserting them. The MacFarlane Home in town is an excellent one. You could even have them out on weekends if you wished and you could visit them frequently. I don't think you realize just what you're saddling my son with, financially."

Lindsay's gray eyes suddenly went green. "Ah, that's it, isn't it! The crux of the whole matter. Money. The most important thing in life to you. You reckon up everything in terms of bawbees. There'll be enough from the sale of the cottage to educate the children, if that's what you're thinking of. I'm only asking for a roof over their heads, their keep. There will be enough for their clothes. And you know full well that the children will almost earn their keep. Look how good Morag is with poultry. Look how wonderful Callum is with sheep and pigs. Mrs. Lockhart, please! Don't you really think this is a matter between Robin and

5

myself? It will only affect us."

The mouth set like a trap. "I'm not willing that the money I worked for so hard should be squandered on the bairns of a ne'er-do-well."

"It won't be your money. Robin only takes the share left him by his father. And he's buying Alastair out. That leaves a third of the farm to draw your income from."

"But the house is still, in effect, mine. I'll keep my foothold in it."

Lindsay, despairing, said gently, "Mrs. Lockhart, if you hadn't wanted to move out, we could have built ourselves a little place — plenty of young couples do just that — and have had the children with us in that. I hate quarreling, but I'll have to repeat what I said, this is between Robin and me."

The black eyes, beady and shrewd, narrowed. "What makes you so sure Robin will want them?"

"Robin has always liked the children. He's been like a big brother to them."

Mrs. Lockhart's laugh had no merriment in it, only malice. "You don't know men very well, Lindsay Macrae. He liked them well enough when they were not his responsibility. But he doesna want them like millstones around his neck."

"I think," said Lindsay with dignity, "that you'll have to let Robin speak for himself."

"He has already spoken to me about it."

Lindsay looked up sharply. "Or have you spoken to him?"

"That's one and the same thing."

"It isn't really. I'd prefer that Robin tell me himself, not have it second hand. I'll go and find him now."

"Aye, do just that." Mrs. Lockhart's voice was as bland as cream. Uneasiness prickled under Lindsay's skin. But that was foolish. She must trust Robin.

Mrs. Lockhart added: "He's up by the Rough Acre. He'll tell you."

★ ★ ★

He did.

Lindsay didn't even get it all out. She said, panting a little, because it was something of a climb, "Oh, Robin. I've been talking to your mother about

7

Callum and Morag. I'm a little upset, you see — "

He came to her, took her hand. "You'll get over it, Lindsay. A bit hard to get used to right away — the idea — but given time you'll see it's best for them. After all, it wasn't your fault your mother married again and picked such a weak character. You can't be saddled with the results of that union for the rest of your life, and neither can I. I had a talk with the master of the home yesterday. They've got a double vacancy in one of the cottages. It's not like an old-time orphanage, you know. It's run on the most modern lines with a married couple in charge of each cottage making it like a perfectly ordinary household."

He waited for her to speak, then said, "Lindsay, what are you looking at me like that for?"

"Like what?" asked Lindsay clearly.

"Like . . . like . . . well, as if you'd never seen me before!"

"I'm just wondering if I ever have, Robin. Or if I've built up an image of you in my heart that doesn't exist at all. A kind, sturdy-spirited mate I could lean on. One for whom my troubles would be his troubles. I can't believe this, Robin, can't believe it's really happening. I've always known your mother was a hard woman, that she rules your life and Alastair's with an iron hand. I even thought I might be able to make up to you for that, when we were married. I thought you had in you what Alastair revealed he had when he cut adrift. Perhaps you haven't."

He had reddened a little. "Lindsay, don't be so high and mighty. It's a matter of common sense. It's — "

"Common sense! When did common sense warm the heart? When did it shield the fatherless? It's not common sense that's needed, Robin, it's bigheartedness. What is there in it? They're good youngsters, helpful around the farm. They'd earn their keep.

"I know you said once, Robin, how lucky you were getting a farmhand for a wife, but I won't always be able to do a full day's work outside. I'll have inside duties and, later, a family to look after. I'd have preferred us to be quite on our own, but children don't upset the matrimonial dovecote much. A month ago the future seemed so uncomplicated. Mother was here, seemingly well, certainly as gay as ever. She — "

"She ought to have told you, Lindsay, that she might go at any time. It wouldn't have been such a shock, then. You'd have put serious thought into the future instead of being incapable of seeing that it isn't right to saddle a man with two children. After all, the farm's been divided into three as it is, and it needn't have been if you had pressed mother to stay on."

Lindsay caught her breath. "Robin! It was for you as much as for me. Look how Alastair has proved himself. He's a different person. I wanted to see you prove yourself a man too, make your own decisions. I've always seen you as you could be . . . unsupported. Even now I'm longing for you to say, 'Of course we'll have the youngsters — their home is with us.'

"You know perfectly well the farm's doing well enough. It could do better — your mother opposes every innovation. Any suggestion I've ever made has been

10

turned down, yet I've only made those suggestions based on what we've tried and proved at Crombie's. But she just sits and says, 'It's never been done before at Strathluan.' If everybody had answered like that all through the ages, we'd still be wearing skins and living in caves!"

Robin set his jaw. "You'd better realize, once and for all, Lindsay, that I have no intention of going against my mother or of taking on another man's children. You approved of Alastair's moving out, getting married against mother's wishes. She cut him out of her will the next day. I don't intend that to happen to me."

Lindsay was so still she didn't appear to be breathing. The impact was too great to be taken in quickly. Then she moved, swaying a little, so that Robin put out a hand to her. She drew back sharply.

"No, Robin, don't touch me." She gave a little laugh. "Well, at last I've realized what I've blinded myself to all along. Something I suspected but wouldn't face up to. You've got that same mercenary streak in you that your mother has. You aren't like your father at all. Your father knew, didn't he? That's why he left the farm in three sections, well tied up. To safeguard Alastair from you both. How wise he was, but how sad for him.

"I wonder if he only found out how mean your mother was after he was married — too late. Well, thank heaven I've found out in time. There's nothing worse than a mean husband. I don't want to make the mistake my mother made . . . I want a man who doesn't shirk responsibility, who takes the rough with the smooth, a man to ride the water with . . . but it isn't you, Robin!"

With one swift movement her ring was off, she lifted his work-stained hand, palm upward, deposited her engagement ring in it, said, fighting back tears, "I'll solve my own problems, Robin, *somehow*," and ran swiftly downhill.

It wasn't till the shoulder of the hill took her out of sight that she stopped. She leaned against a mountain ash, its leaves turning russet, and tried to regain her breath, to prevent sobs escaping. She mustn't go in to the children with reddened eyelids.

12

They were only just beginning to get over the loss of their mother. So was Lindsay. You had to. You had to go on with life. That had been in the letter mother had left, telling her that for two years she had known she might go at any time, owing to a heart condition, though she had hoped that she might, as so many did, live for years, with medical aid. She hadn't wanted any shadow of impending parting hanging over their lives, she hadn't wanted them to cosset her, had wanted to go on earning till the cottage was paid off.

'Give them a happy childhood, Lindsay,' the letter had gone on.

Through an error of judgment on my part they've never known a father's love. If I do go, Lindsay, you'll have to let Lex know. I've put his address at the bottom. It's only fair that he should know he is free. But the children will be safe with you and Robin. God bless you, darling.

With you and Robin.
Lindsay stayed against the tree, giving

13

herself breathing space before going down into the village to meet a problem that yesterday she had not imagined existed. What could she do?

James Crombie had said to her only yesterday, "I think you and Robin should hurry up your wedding, lass. This is wearing you down, chasing home after milking, worrying your life out lest the bairns get into mischief between school and your homecoming, getting up early so's to be here on time."

She'd said: "You're right, Mr. Crombie. Besides, it's hardly fair to you. With winter approaching I won't be able to stay so long. Farmhands ought to live in. But I have to be home before dark, they're not old enough to be left for long. Besides, the cottage still carries a mortgage, and now there's only one wage coming in it won't stretch far enough. I think Robin and I must be married before Christmas."

Mrs. Crombie had joined in. "Aye . . . but be careful of one thing. See if you can hustle up Robin's mother. That house of hers in town has been ready this long while. Dinna take the bairns to live wi' that one. She's meaner than second skimmings."

What *could* she do?

Lindsay felt a wave of despair sweep over her, and repulsed it. She must not panic. Mother had survived worse than this.

Lindsay thought of her stepfather, Alexander Bairdmore, of his sheep station across the world in New Zealand. It wasn't right he should have got off scot-free, that Lindsay's lovely mother should have worked herself to death to support his children.

Lindsay's eyes grew dark with remembered pain, with the knowledge of the anguish her mother must have suffered.

Her mother had said, "If I had married him for his money, Lindsay, it would have served me right, but I didn't. I loved him. It was like a miracle. I'd been widowed so young, I'd thought never to love again. Then Lex came. He was having a year in Scotland, visiting the land of his forebears. Auntie Jean offered to take you, she loved you so, of course. What a wonderful three months we had. France, Italy, Switzerland, Germany, Norway,

15

Sweden, Spain . . .

"Then back here while Lex traveled all over Scotland. I went with him at first, but then I wasn't well. The twins were coming. The doctor advised me against traveling to New Zealand till after the baby was born. We didn't dream of two, of course. I didn't expect him to stay glued to my side. I had you and Auntie Jean. Then suddenly I went blind. It was a terrible shock. They didn't suspect it was only to do with the kidney trouble I had developed during the pregnancy.

"Jean sent for Lex. He was appalled. I thought naturally it was on my account. I didn't realize he couldn't take the thought of being tied for life to a blind woman. Lindsay, I came up from a pleasant dream into a nightmare. Your father had been so different. We'd had quite a struggle when we first married, but it hadn't mattered. We'd enjoyed our pinching and scraping, our shabby makeshifts. And how we had enjoyed you!

"I began to notice the change in Lex's voice, his withdrawal, the change in his personality. I told him I was sure that

16

we could adjust ourselves, that as soon
as the baby was born we'd go to New
Zealand, that Jean was prepared to come
with us, that she would look after you
and the new baby and Lex's son Neill.
Isn't it odd, I've always had a yearning
after Lex's Neill? Then — then one
morning Lex was gone. He must have
laid his plans well ahead. It wasn't
sudden impulse, for you don't get away
from one country to another as easily
as that.

"He left a note, stating quite baldly
that he couldn't face looking after a
blind wife for the rest of his life. He
had left a tidy sum in the local bank
for me, enough to see me through very
comfortably till after the birth of my
baby, and his lawyers would see that I
got a regular income after that.

"Jean and I almost went mad. I don't
know what I'd have done without her. I
had to sink my pride and take that money.
We couldn't have managed without. It
was the disillusionment that was hardest
to bear, Lindsay. But for you, I'd not
have cared whether I lived or died.
Indeed, because I felt I was going to

17

be a drag on everyone, I prayed that I might die and my baby with me. Jean got me out of that slough of despair. She went on teaching here. But oh, Lindsay, the miracle of seeing again! I felt I'd never ask any more of life than that.

"They'd brought the babies to me, put them in my arms. I turned my head a little, feeling that I would put my cheek against their downy little heads and, suddenly, was aware that I could see them, the dark one like Lex, the ginger one like me. Not well, only dimly, but I could see them! Perhaps I should have written Lex to tell him I had regained my sight, that he had a son and a daughter, but I couldn't. Something had snapped in me. I couldn't have lived with a man I despised. His lawyer sent a lump sum every year. By the time the twins were five I started teaching again and told the lawyer I didn't want to take any more money. I felt the twins were mine, never Lex's. I was afraid to keep in touch even that much, lest in later years he came to Scotland again and might claim the children, weaning them away from me with money. You'll remember him, of course, Lindsay? After all, you were twelve when I married him."

"Yes, I remember him well, mother." She had stooped and kissed her mother. "I remember how charming he was. I don't wonder you loved him, mother. I did, too, that brief summer, full of comings and goings. Till I grew to hate even the sound of his name for what he did to you. And, mother, I don't say much, but how I admire you, picking up the pieces of your life, being so gay and gallant, never letting on to the twins that their father was a rotter. Even when Auntie Jean died you hardly faltered. I wish I could have made it up to you."

"You have, Lindsay. You've been all a daughter could be. So like your father. And you've been so wonderful with Callum and Morag. If ever anything happened to me, I'd have no fears for them because of you."

Lindsay had laughed, flicked her mother under the chin, said gaily, "Bless my boots, we are getting all tragic! Nothing's going to happen, pet. I'll be married next year. I'll ask Robin to let me extend the poultry side of the farm so I can still have an income of my own and be able to continue to help you with the twins' education."

But it hadn't been quite like that, for a month ago Margaret Bairdmore had come home after her day's teaching, sat down, said, "Oh, you've got a cup of tea ready. I do so enjoy your days off. How lovely, Lindsay." And she had sighed, slipped sideways against the head of the couch and left all her responsibilities in this world.

★ ★ ★

Now Lindsay stood on the heather-purple hillside, clenching her hands, willing the tears not to fall.

She could hear her mother's voice in memory, that philosophical, patient voice. 'When one door closes, Lindsay, another opens. Remember that all through life, dear.'

There must be a door, somewhere.

She pulled herself together. There were other things mother had said . . . one was that it was just as well there was always something needing to be done. 'In life's most poignant and despairing moments, there is always the blessing of having to prepare a meal, scrub a floor.'

That was right. The children would so soon be in from school. She must go home. This was her precious day off when the evening meal need not be hurried. She would make them griddle cakes, they loved them hot, buttered. She would spread them with rowan jelly. And she would preserve some more eggs and tidy the pantry. Tonight the Rollinsons were coming to look at the cottage. That stabbed. She'd told them it was in the cards she might be getting married sooner. But what now? They must keep a roof over their heads.

But first, the task at hand, the griddle cakes.

But the mail had come. She picked it up in a bunch, took it through to the kitchen, dropped the letters on the table. They spread out fanwise, four white envelopes and a blue airmail letter. She stared at it. The stamp said New Zealand.

She started to shake inside. She picked it up with as much apprehension as if she had been stretching out a tentative hand to a snarling dog.

She had written to Lex Bairdmore a week after her mother's death, by airmail. Her mother had been right, it was only fair he should know he was free. But she didn't want to open that letter. It would bring back, in a bitter flood, all her old resentment at what her mother had suffered.

She slowly took a pair of scissors, slit along two sides, carefully unfolded it.

The address on the back carried the Central Otago one to which she had written. The inside was headed briefly 'Dunedin Public Hospital'. The writing was quite good, not the hand of a very sick man. Something minor in illness, perhaps.

She read:

Dear Lindsay,

You will be surprised to hear from me after all these years. You were a dear little girl and I expect you have harbored hard thoughts of me. I deserve them all. I was most astounded to receive your airmail letter, to know that I had twins, not just one child, and to know that your mother had regained her sight immediately after they were born. Perhaps I saw myself in a true light — as never before — when I realized she had despised me enough never to let me know.

Retribution has visited me, Lindsay. Exactly an hour after I read your letter the specialist told me I will be blind within a month. I must put things right as far as I'm able. Before I started this letter I made a will signed by two of the nursing staff, to make Callum and Morag coheirs with Neill. Neill is a good lad, stronger in character than ever I was, thank God. He will be delighted to have kin of his own. He will be in to see me this weekend and I shall tell him. The station is managed by one Euan Hazeldean, and I have made him Neill's guardian.

I have probably not more than a year to live. I would like to see my children before I die. Also I would like to see you. I would like to be assured of your forgiveness, if you can give it. I feel if you could forgive me, on your

23

mother's behalf, then Margaret would have, too. Will you come, Lindsay, and bring the children? They would have a home. You didn't mention money matters, but I feel it may not be plentiful. There's more than enough for you all at Rhoslochan. It doesn't take long to fly these days. Come soon. I'll see my lawyer and make arrangements for a bank draft for your fares, but perhaps you could set things in motion there. I may not have as much time as I hope. Hoping you will not cherish a justifiable grievance against me, hoping you will help me to ease my conscience,

Alexander Bairdmore
P.S. I'm leaving you a sum of money, too. It's only right.

Lindsay dropped down into a chair, stared unseeingly at the far wall. She felt exactly as if someone had bludgeoned her. It was one shock on top of another.
For a moment a great wave of resentment swept over her. And some other feeling. She wasn't sure what . . . a sense of being caught up in a

24

situation that she didn't like, from which everything within her shrank.

The past rushed back to her . . . mother battling gallantly to support her children, determined they should not suffer too much through an error of hers . . . mother quietly and steadfastly opposed to them ever having anything to do with an unworthy father . . . her grit in sticking to teaching in an effort to make the cottage freehold, till the twins were educated.

'Given time I'll do it,' she had said to Lindsay once.

Time was what she hadn't been given. And now?

Lindsay didn't know.

At that moment she heard the children. She pushed the blue letter under the others, straightened up, said brightly, "Well, you've beaten me to it. I meant to have griddle cakes ready for you to eat with rowan jelly. Never mind, I'll cut you a piece."

Morag's ginger crest was standing up, a sign of excitement.

"Lindsay we've been invited to a party — Jinny Malcolm's. She had told her mother she hadn't wanted one, then just this morning she decided she'd like one after all. So her mother said it must be a party without any frills and without presents, but she's baked all day. And we can go, can't we? It's boys and girls — all our class, no favorites. Say yes, Lindsay!"

Lindsay laughed. It would give her time to think things out.

"Yes, you may go. Only not like that. Both of you wash your hands and faces and knees. And, Callum, no skimping your ears. And you're to stay till I fetch you, do you hear?"

The minute they had banged the gate behind them, it creaked again. She wasn't to have time to decide — it was Mrs. Rollinson.

Her daughter-in-law and son were coming from Canada. How different her attitude from Mrs. Lockhart's.

Mrs. Rollinson said, "Jim thought they could just live with us for a bit. The great ninny! Isn't it going to be hard enough for that girl, leaving her homeland and all her own folk, and wi' two toddlers to boot, wi' out trying to fit into another woman's house? Losh, I couldna ha' stood it when my bairns were small. I wrote and told him we'd get them a cottage and sell it again later if it wasn't what they wanted. In the meantime his wife would be verra thankful for her hearthside where she could spank or spoil her bairns wi'out a mother-in-law butting in."

Mrs. Rollinson said now, "I'm not wishing to hurry you in any decision, Lindsay lass, but we've an option on Johnsons' and it's just till tomorrow. I'd rather have this. Johnsons' mebbe is more modern, but this is prettier, and if I'm any judge of Stephanie from her letters, it's what she'll want. But my husband, manlike, wanted to check about the roof and the drains, so I thought I'd ask you first, and if it's convenient the plumber'll go over them tomorrow morn.

"We'll no' be wanting it till after Christmas, you ken, but we must know because of this option. I thought it could be that you and Robin might be speeding up your wedding like . . . with this happening, and that being a heaven-sent solution to where the bairns can bide and you home all day to look after them."

Automatically Lindsay's hand came to cover where her ring had been. Mrs. Rollinson was as shrewd as she was kindly, and the absence of the ring, plus a tiny graze where Lindsay had wrenched it off, would be a case of two and two.

She swallowed. "It — it's not decided yet, what we're going to do, Mrs. Rollinson, but I'll let you know tomorrow one way or another. I'll decide things tonight."

Mrs. Rollinson nodded sagely. "Robin will be coming down. Now about this roof . . . "

She stayed an hour, and as soon as she was gone, it rushed back on Lindsay. She read the letter over again, slowly.

Her first feeling of recoil from it was receding, pity taking its place. Lex Bairdmore was face to face with reality now — something he couldn't run away from. And he wanted to put things straight, to square his accounts.

She didn't want anything to do with him, but what must it be like to be facing blindness and death with that on your conscience? To ask forgiveness, to have it refused? If she said she forgave him but refused to go he'd feel she hadn't forgiven. But how were the children going to react to the news that they had a father? A father who was dying, who had deserted them when they were helpless infants? What was she going to tell them?

A wave of anger swept Lindsay. It was just another complication. If only she could write back offering forgiveness but saying that as she was about to be married she could not come, it would simplify matters. Oh, Robin, Robin!

And was this . . . could this be the door her mother said would open? Pride was all very well, but when you were poor you could not afford the luxury of pride. Could she deny the children their rightful heritage, the opportunities of a better education? Yet how could she uproot them, go right across the world to the man who had ruined her mother's life?

If only she had more time to decide — but houses in this village were hard to sell, more people were leaving Feadan than coming in. Lindsay lifted her head, looked at the clock. In a few moments she must go for the children. It was dark.

The next moment they were flying up the path, banging open the door. Lindsay got up, ready to scold them for not waiting, then stopped. Callum was chalk white, Morag flushed and bright eyed.

The tears spilled out as she spoke. "Lindsay, it isn't true, is it? Tell us it isn't true. We aren't going into the MacFarlane, are we? We're not, are we? Maggie Murray said we were. She heard Mrs. Lockhart saying so. That you couldn't keep us here and Robin wouldn't have us . . . Lindsay, we — "

Lindsay gathered her close, looked over her head, met the intensity of Callum's gaze. She shook her head. "Of course you aren't! How ridiculous! What's Mrs. Lockhart got to do with us? I'm not even marrying Robin. How could you go into an orphanage when you've got a sister. Think how lonely I'd be. The way people get hold of the wrong story! We're all going to New Zealand!"

2

SHE wrote a letter that night. It took her into the wee sma's. She tore up three before she was satisfied. She assured Lex Bairdmore of her forgiveness, and told him she was selling the cottage and would make flight reservations with what was left when the mortgage was repaid. He could recompense them for it when they arrived — it would save time and might be awkward for him when he was in hospital.

I would rather come by ship, of course, it would set the children up, but in view of what you told me of your health, it will need to be air. So many people are emigrating, it was in the news lately that sea passages have to be booked at least eighteen months ahead. It costs much more, but I gather you won't mind that. I haven't told the children what happened years ago — merely that you and mother parted. It will be up to you to see that they have nice memories of you. I do sincerely trust that your health may improve, despite what the doctors say, and I'll do all in my power to assist you.

She couldn't help a faint doubt in her own mind as to her stepfather's motives. With no woman relative, he might easily think his stepdaughter would be an asset to help him bear his affliction. Well, she supposed she could help, at that. One must not return evil for evil.

Things fell into place, events moved smoothly. Lindsay was wryly amused when Mrs. Lockhart arrived to make the peace. She hinted that Lindsay might come back . . . presumably the richer and that the half brother and guardian might take the children.

"Families should be united," she purred. "This guardian and his wife might easily make a home for them. What a wonderful chance for the children, growing up in a young country, inheriting a fine estate. And have no qualms about this legacy, Lindsay. It's your due and more. The children have cost you a pretty penny."

Lindsay was icily distant. "I won't be coming back, Mrs. Lockhart. I won't be leaving the children. I believe in families being united too, you see. I've no idea what manner of man this guardian of Neill's is, even, and I've nothing to come back for."

"You have Robin. This was only a little tiff, a misunderstanding."

"On the contrary, Mrs. Lockhart, I understood only too well. And I understand this, too . . . you think I'm coming into money, and everything you say makes the possibility of a reconciliation even more remote. I've no desire to marry into a family like yours."

Robin came too, that night, came with the easy assurance that he could put matters right but went away with his ears red. Lindsay let him go without a pang, except for wishing that she might have fallen in love with a man who'd have stood by her when she had most needed him. In her mother's life she had seen the need to judge character wisely in the matter of a life partner. She felt drained of emotion but firmly resolved to build a new life in the Southern Hemisphere, unhampered by regrets.

Alexander Bairdmore sent her a telegram.

Delighted to have you all. Let me have flight details by air as soon as possible. Will have you met Dunedin Airport. God bless.

Bairdmore.

The 'God bless' warmed Lindsay's heart. Lex Bairdmore seemed a changed man. She must accept that, be prepared to forget the past. She still doubted if last-minute repentance in an ill-spent life counted for much, but one could not entirely write it off. It might be genuine.

They got an earlier flight than expected. Lindsay took it and wrote airmail to let her stepfather know. She had been tempted to cable, but it would have been lengthy and costly; and till she knew how things stood financially, she must husband her resources. She still had a lingering distrust of Lex Bairdmore. But she repressed the thought. After all, her stepfather hadn't even waited to hear from her without getting a new will signed. She must not let the children guess she was worried; they must have security. She must not dim their delighted anticipation of the trip. They must look forward to meeting their father and half brother. There might be many adjustments and setbacks ahead of them. Neill might regard them as usurpers, though if the children themselves were perfectly natural that would be disarming, and the chances were fairly good, especially if they realized Lindsay was willing to pull her weight with the nursing.

Things had gone well with the bookings. She must take that as an omen for the future and she might as well enjoy the wonderful plane trip ahead.

At San Francisco a telegram was brought to her. Oddly enough, it had been sent to Scotland first. But — but her stepfather had known the time she was leaving. Apprehension clutched tight fingers about Lindsay's heart. She read the message; dropped it, picked it up with almost nerveless fingers, read it again.

It wasn't signed by her stepfather. It was addressed 'Lindsay Macrae' and read:

Regret to inform you Lex Bairdmore died on 24th. Strongly advise you stay in Scotland till you hear from his lawyers. No point coming here now.

Euan Hazeldean.

Lindsay turned swiftly away so that the airport officials should not see her face. Callum and Morag, fortunately, were buying postcards at the stationery counter to send to school friends.

So she had acted too hastily. She could have stayed home and had a certain income, even capital, perhaps, coming to the children. Yet, even if that was so, she could not have refused the plea of a dying man to see his children. All she could do was go on. Lex must have died before her letter with the flight dates reached them. They would know now that she was on her way.

★ ★ ★

Lindsay may have harbored doubts before, but now she knew even more when she thought about her landing. There was no one now in this strange land, no link with the old.

But she must not panic. Her stepfather had said the manager was a fine man. He and the lawyer would help her. She wished she knew more of the setup at Rhoslochan. Probably the manager and his family lived in a house on the sheep station. Would her stepfather have had a housekeeper looking after himself and Neill? Might there be a place for her there, looking after the children, perhaps helping outside if the housekeeper didn't want assistance inside?

The news affected the children very little. Lindsay was with them, and that was all that mattered.

At last the Viscount was hovering over Momona, where Dunedin Airport was situated. Below them lay a fair green land, intersected by rivers, a land of huge, upflung mountains, rolling hills far as the eye could see, reaching back into the hinterland which, a fellow traveler told them, was Central Otago, where they would be living.

To the east stretched a peninsula, guarding the harbor waters; beyond that was the open sea with surf creaming at its edge, the pacific. Beyond that, south, what? Only the icy wastes of the South Pole, she supposed.

They came down, the passengers began to stir. There were no formalities here, of course, as there had been at Christchurch Airport, no customs to go through.

They gathered their things together; the luggage would be taken into the terminal building. Lindsay's heart began to thump. In a few moments, she supposed, the children would meet their half brother, the manager, the lawyer.

They crossed the runway and went inside. All around them people were greeting each other, lucky, lucky people who were not alone in the world, people who could recognize the folk they were to meet. Her eyes scanned the people in the big lounge.

She rejected group after group. There

would be two men and a youth, or one man and a youth. Or would the manager's wife come with him? Nice if she did. They stood hesitantly, looking about them, Morag, of course, talking nineteen to the dozen.

"Quiet, Morag, please. No, it couldn't possibly be that group. I can't see any — "

Suddenly a man came toward them. He was what Mrs. Rollinson would have called black avised. His face was lean, rather hawklike, with deep lines engraved in the cheeks, he was tanned to almost a brick color and he had overhanging brows above dark hazel eyes.

He wore no hat. He said, halting in front of them and looking piercingly at the children, "I rather think these could be the children I'm looking for — I noticed a Scots accent — but if so, I'm wondering where their guardian is. I'm expecting to meet a Mr. Lindsay Macrae and two children. Are these — "

Lindsay said incredulously, *"Mister* Lindsay Macrae! *I'm Lindsay Macrae.* These are the twins, Callum and Morag Bairdmore. Can you be — "

"Euan Hazeldean, yes. But how can you be a girl?"

"Mainly because I was born a girl, I suppose." Lindsay's tone was tart. "What mix-up is this? Surely my stepfather gave you to understand his wife had a *daughter* by her first marriage!"

He was scowling fiercely. "We didn't know anything about you. We knew he had contracted an unfortunate marriage on that trip of his to Scotland all those years ago. But he never mentioned a stepchild till just before he died."

Lindsay bent swiftly to the children. "There's another plane coming in. Like to go up on the balcony and watch? Mr. Hazeldean and I will sort this out. Funny, isn't it? Mr. Hazeldean thinking I was a man! Off you go."

They hesitated, sensing something wrong, but a little reassured by the lightness of her tone.

Callum said sturdily, "Lindsay, will you be all right?"

Lindsay managed a smile. "Of course. It's just a stupid mistake. Now off with you or you'll miss it. Don't come down till I call you."

Euan Hazeldean said, "Well, at least they're obedient."

A spark lit Lindsay's eye. "What did you expect them to be? Savages?"

"I could have expected anything. I'm not at all impressed by the way you dashed out here the moment you knew Neill's father had only a certain time to live. Reminds one of vultures gathering."

Lindsay had never felt more angry in her life.

She managed, "I came because my stepfather requested it. I didn't want to see him again. I didn't even respect him."

"Poor Lex! No stepfather has an easy time, I imagine, but you must have done nothing to improve the situation."

She lifted her chin, looked directly at him, her gray eyes stone-cold and sober.

"Mr. Hazeldean, you didn't know enough of the situation to even know my sex. Do you know why my mother and Lex Bairdmore parted?"

"I do. He told me the whole story."

She was puzzled. "Then what did you think of him coming back to

41

New Zealand like that? Should he not have stayed with her? Surely you don't approve?"

"What else could a man do? A farmer needs a wife who can pull her weight. So what?"

She was temporarily bereft of speech. Then, "Well, all I can say is that if you and my stepfather are typical of New Zealand men I'm sorry we came. And the mistake about my sex is ridiculous. You must be really dim!"

He said stiffly, "I addressed my first telegram to Lindsay Macrae. Your stepfather took this turn for the worse suddenly. His mind was a little clouded. He sent for me, told me the whole story, said his wife had a child by her first marriage — Lindsay Macrae. He said Lindsay was the guardian of his children, but he would make me a co-guardian. He said you would be leaving Scotland soon. He must have been a little confused. We thought you hadn't yet left. Your cabled answer from San Francisco was also signed Lindsay."

"Of course. It's a girl's name as well as a boy's. Surely you knew that? Like

Beverly, Jocelyn and Leslie."

"Yes, but just as Leslie is L-E-Y in the case of a girl, so Lindsay is usually S-E-Y, surely?"

"Yes, that's so. But I was named for my mother's family, who were Lindsays. I can see now how it occurred. Still, that was not my fault, and what does it matter that I'm a woman and not a man?"

"It matters a lot. You can't stay at Rhoslochan."

"Why not? Oh, do you mean that you live in the big house and it would upset your wife to have another woman about the place?"

"I mean there is no woman. I'm not married. Neill and I live alone there. There's just one other cottage on the estate. It's not a fabulous place, you know. And the cottage isn't big enough for you to board there. I'm adding on a couple of rooms as it is. The wife comes up and cooks our dinner for us. This is a serious complication, your being a woman."

Lindsay's legs felt as unsubstantial as cotton wool. Why hadn't Lex Bairdmore explained the situation? Or had he expected to live his year out, to be there with them? What a ghastly muddle!

She looked up. "Is there a village nearby? Could we stay in it, temporarily at least? I have enough to carry me for the moment, and I suppose when things get settled, I can call on the estate?"

"On the estate?" He looked at her sharply.

"Yes, of course. When my stepfather first approached me he said he'd made out a new will — immediately he'd known he hadn't long to live. Naturally he wanted to make things right for his children. He said the children would be joint heirs with Neill. They're just as much his children as Neill is, Mr. Hazeldean. And I'm here to protect their interests. I suppose that will was found?"

He said slowly, reluctantly, she thought, "Yes, it was found. In his locker. I passed it on to the lawyer. But — "

"Then there isn't much left to be said, except that I must see this lawyer. I suppose I can see him today. I expected him here to meet me. Then we can travel to Central Otago and I'll find board nearby."

44

"You can't. There isn't even a township. Or near neighbors. In any case I wouldn't want you with neighbors. It would cause talk. You'll have to stay at Rhoslochan. I'll sleep in the *whare*."

"In the warry?"

"A hut. We use them for shearers. *Whare* is Maori word meaning house or hut. It's in common use here. It will do for a day or two, but — "

"No more buts, please. I'm getting tired of them. These children have traveled right across the world. They lost their mother just seven weeks ago. I don't want them to feel unwanted. I didn't tell them why mother and my stepfather parted. I just said the marriage hadn't worked out. I would like them to meet Neill without any resentment in their hearts."

"Resentment? Why the devil should — "

"Neill's had his birthright all these years. But let's not discuss that now. I must get the children. There's nothing for them to see now and they'll get restless, perhaps even uneasy. It wasn't much of a welcome. Where do we go from here? We seem surrounded by

45

fields. Where is Dunedin? I'd like to see that lawyer right away."

"Why?"

"Isn't it obvious? To know exactly where we stand."

His expression was forbidding, grim in the extreme. "It might not be convenient for him at so short notice."

Lindsay looked disbelieving. "When he knows what a distance we have to go? Oh, come! Tell me his name and I'll call him, make an appointment for as early as possible this afternoon. I'll try not to hold you up any longer than possible. But I must see him."

"I'll call him for you, from town. We'll go into Dunedin now, have some lunch."

"I would like to call him myself, thank you, if you'll tell me his name. How long will it take us to get to the city?"

"Just over half an hour. But I'll call. I'll explain the situation a little."

Lindsay's brown brows twitched together. "I'll do the explaining myself. It doesn't seem to have been done well till now."

"That's quite unjust, and is hard, to

46

boot. We were dealing with a dying man, remember. He had a brain tumor."

Lindsay bit her lip. She rallied. "I was trying to match hardness with hardness. You sounded anything but sentimental earlier — even upholding Lex's attitude towards my mother."

"I don't think it would profit us to discuss that, Miss Macrae. It belongs to other years. And now, in fairness to the children who, I admit, are the innocent parties in all this, we'd better let it appear we have our cross-purposes straightened out."

They walked toward the staircase, beckoned the children.

They looked a little apprehensive as they came toward Lindsay and the manager.

Before Lindsay could speak he did. "Well, we've got it all unsnarled. I should have remembered Lindsay could be a girl's name too. We're going into Dunedin. Know what that means, that name? Edin on the hills. Named after Edinburgh. We'll have some lunch and I'll fix up an appointment for your sister to see your father's lawyer, then when we go to see him I'll drop you children at the Museum — how would you like that? You could study the native birds perhaps, if you're interested in such things, and then be able to identify them around Rhoslochan. And we'll set off for Central not later than four if possible. It's a fairish step."

The children were all for it. Morag beamed at him. Lindsay straightened her sailor hat, smoothed her elfin locks back . . . if there was such a thing as a ginger elf.

Callum looked directly at Euan Hazeldean. "Where is my brother?" he asked. It gave Lindsay a strange feeling.

"At school. A district high school. He'd have loved to be here, but as it's November they're sitting exams, and he'd lost a bit of schooling with his father's — your father's — death."

"He's nearly sixteen, isn't he?" asked Callum. "What does he look like?"

Euan Hazeldean grinned. "Like you. No more, no less."

He got their luggage, stowed it in a luxurious estate car he called a station wagon, opened the front door for the children to sit by him, the rear door for Lindsay. She felt it emphasized the fact that she was the outsider.

As he started the engine he looked down on Morag. "Do you know what?" he asked her.

Morag shook her head. "No . . . what?"

"If there's one thing I like above all others it's freckles!"

Really, the man sounded almost human. Morag beamed at him again, but Lindsay wondered if she would ever feel relaxed, settled, again. If she would ever feel at home anywhere, secure, loved, happy.

The children's chatter bridged any awkwardness. "Oh, just like Edinburgh," cried Callum. "See Lindsay, Princes Street, fancy that!"

The manager's dark face creased into a smile. "Not only that but George Street, too . . . Heriot Row, Hanover Street, Queen Street, Water of Leith . . . and, of course, Robbie Burns sitting gathering moss in the Octagon."

He drew up at a hotel, took them in. Perhaps it wasn't to be compared with the best British hotels, but it was so far removed from the world of Callum and Morag that what they thought amounted to magnificence awed them into an unnatural silence.

Callum broke it to say in a reverent tone, "My goodness, we really must've come into money! I must say it's a nice change after having to be so careful of money always."

Lindsay saw Mr. Hazeldean's mouth tighten and felt her color rise.

He sat them down. They ordered soup, then he rose and said swiftly, "I'll just call MacWilson now. Otherwise he'll leave for lunch." He left Lindsay sitting fuming. She could hardly pursue him to the phone or argue in front of hotel staff that she wanted to speak to the lawyer herself.

He had known that and taken her by surprise. Something that wasn't yet suspicion, more a deep uneasiness, gave Lindsay a fluttery feeling in the pit of her stomach. Certainly, in addition to being farm manager he was also Neill's guardian, but — the soup arrived. The children tucked in.

Lindsay found she was enjoying it. The food on the aircraft had been delicious, even luxurious, but it was good to be eating on firm earth again. Euan Hazeldean was a long time.

Meticulously, she covered his soup with a side plate. He must not find her lacking in consideration. They had started their fish before he returned.

"Oh, thank you," he said, uncovering his soup.

Lindsay's eyes lifted to his face. "You were a long time," she said pointedly.

"Aye. It took some explaining."

"Did it now? I'd have thought it was basically simple. Merely 'Lindsay Macrae is a woman, not a man. Seems we misunderstood. She wants to see you this afternoon if possible before we leave!'"

He shook his head, unsmiling. "We found a lot to discuss in that. As it was I had to remind Jim that my soup would probably be stone-cold."

Lindsay raised her delicately winged eyebrows. " Jim? Oh, you mean the lawyer? Good gracious, I'd heard New Zealanders were very casual, particularly in the matter of Christian names — but I didn't realize it would extend to business relations, too."

He looked hatefully amused. "It's not as a lawyer I call Jim by his first name, but because I've known him since schooldays when I was a small third grader and he was head prefect. Since then I've caught up a bit, so that we're more like contemporaries."

"I see," said Lindsay.

He put down his spoon. "You said that very meaningfully. As if something lay behind it. What?"

The gray eyes went guileless. "Just that I saw why you called him by his Christian name."

She didn't think he was satisfied, but he let it go. Something in Lindsay stood guard. So the lawyer was a personal friend, was he?

They left the children at the museum in Great King Street and drove to Dowling Street.

James MacWilson was in his late thirties, she thought. Lindsay, trying to be honest, didn't know if he were really suave, or if, prejudiced already against him, she only thought him that.

He chaffed her easily about the mistake they had made saying, "Jock here tells me

52

he nearly dropped in his tracks when he discovered his coguardian was a girl. I tell him he's got all the luck. Oh well, we could trace the mistake all right. Lex only mentioned a child by his wife's former marriage and he was wandering in his mind that day, so we had great difficulty keeping him to the subject. In fact, he'd been confused for some time."

"Had he, indeed?" asked Lindsay clearly. She understood the trend of the conversation. "But his first letter showed no trace of that. It was exceptionally well composed — I thought at the time, because of that, that perhaps he was not as ill as he thought he was, and that I might be able to nurse him."

Mr. MacWilson said quickly. "We're not suggesting that his mind was confused when he sent for you. Oh, no, but — "

"And he told me then that he had made the will providing for his twin son and daughter, as well as for Neill, *before* he wrote the letter, that two members of the nursing staff had witnessed it, so that, too, must have been written when he was fully aware of what he was doing."

She caught Mr. MacWilson and Euan

Hazeldean exchanging a meaningful glance. She wished she could read it, nevertheless there was unease in it, of that she was sure.

"Of course, and as his lawyer, I'm here to see that my late client's wishes are carried out. You need have no fear as to the children's future, Miss Macrae. They're well provided for. Their education, housing, keep, everything will be provided out of the estate. The matter of capital will, of course, be in abeyance till they come of age. They will be treated in every way as Neill is."

Smooth, very smooth. Lindsay thanked him. She would have to reserve her suspicions till she could delve further. The main thing now was to take up residence at Rhoslochan and find out for herself how things stood.

On the surface they appeared straight-forward. The will was read to her. Things were as Lex Bairdmore had promised — equally divided among the three children. At the end, James MacWilson looked across at her. "All satisfactory, I think?"

Lindsay had a line between her brows.

She would have to ask it.

"In a postscript to his letter, my stepfather said he would make a legacy available to me. There isn't any mention of it."

"He must have changed his mind," said the lawyer. "I'm so sorry, but no legacies are mentioned at all."

Lindsay had to accept that. There was nothing she could do. Just another of Lex Bairdmore's pie-crust promises. Not that she had wanted his money, but she had given up her own earning opportunities to bring the children here to their inheritance. What a situation! And she was not welcome at the homestead because she was a woman and the conventions must be observed.

There was to be an account established for Callum and Morag on which she could draw for their needs, an account to be supervised by the lawyer himself and the detestable Euan Hazeldean. Lindsay dared say nothing against this. She didn't know the legal position. Galling as it would be to have to consult the manager about items of personal expenditure for the children, she must concede him his right as their coguardian. If she opposed him at all it might turn out that though their mother had made her, Lindsay, her children's guardian, it might be able to be set aside in favor of a father's wishes. Lindsay felt she needed time to assess the whole situation.

She rose, thanked them for putting the situation before her, turned to go, swung around again, and caught the two men exchanging a look of great relief. They both hastily looked away.

MacWilson said, "Well, goodbye, Jock. Sorry not to have had you for longer, perhaps you'll stay the night with us next time."

As they went down the stairs, Lindsay, to break the silence, said: "He called you Jock. Is your second name John?"

"No . . . all Hazeldeans end up Jocks. Just as all Rhodes are called Dusty. Merely a nickname. Everyone calls me Jock."

"Jock . . . Hazeldean?" said Lindsay uncertainly. "Oh, now I get it. Sir Walter Scott's poem. Jock of Hazeldean." She couldn't help it. She giggled.

"What's so funny?" His tone wasn't

offended, only curious.

She sobered up. "Just that it's so romantic a poem. The lady weeping by the tide for Jock of Hazeldean. 'But aye she loot the tears down fa' for Jock of Hazeldean.' I think Euan suits you much better. A rougher-hewn sort of name."

To herself she added, *Grim, dour, and the rest*.

Euan Hazeldean merely looked bored. "Anyway, there was no thought of pleasing you when I was christened."

"Hardly. You must be old enough to be my father."

Startled, he stopped on the stair, looked at her, then chuckled. "You're just trying to be provoking. I'm thirty-two and you are about twenty-two or three, I'd say. I find that amusing. It's just because you're chagrined at having no legacy."

Lindsay clenched her fists, lifted her chin, said, "I am not! I never wanted anything from my stepfather. When he wrote I wanted to refuse to come. But you can't afford grand gestures like that when you have two children and no means of supporting them."

"You mean your mother got through

it all? She didn't invest any for the years ahead of the youngsters?"

"Invest? What was there to invest? She had her salary as a teacher, nothing more. We only just got by on it with my wages. We never even managed to pay off the cottage. We had ten years to go, and mother didn't live that long."

He gripped her by the arm. "But what about the allowance Lex paid her for the children? I know he thought there was only one, but — "

"My mother, through a lawyer — presumably not this one — took an allowance for only the first five years of their lives, till they went to school, and she could go back to teaching. We managed fine while my Aunt Jean lived with us, after she died it wasn't so easy. But we managed."

The dark hazel eyes bored into hers. "Are you telling the truth?"

"I'm in the habit of it. Mother wouldn't take any more money than she absolutely had to, from him."

"Well, that was something," he muttered.

"What did you say?"

He made an impatient gesture. "Never mind — it doesn't matter — but I wonder where the money went."

"What do you mean?"

He looked away, studied the toe of his shoe, tracing a pattern on the stairway.

She repeated her question.

"Just that — oh well, I'd have thought his estate would have been larger. Then I thought if he'd been supporting two children as well as a wife in a separate establishment all these years that would account for it."

Lindsay blinked. Something had occurred to her. She spoke the thought aloud. "How strange . . . in our interview with the lawyer, he didn't mention how much the estate does amount to. Should I not know — as the children's guardian?"

"Their coguardian," he amended. He went on, and Lindsay thought he was picking his words with great care. It did not imbue her with a feeling of trust.

"I don't think you know much about such legal processes do you? It's not like where an estate is sold up. Then it can be reckoned in terms of pounds, shillings and pence. The value of this estate lies not in its bank balance, which fluctuates terrifically with wool sales and harvest yields. It lies in its acres, its machinery, its potential assets. I think you'll have to be satisfied with the income the children will draw from the estate. There is no capital in actual cash, but the estate will be wisely managed and administered."

"That will do in the meantime," said Lindsay.

It would have to. She knew nothing of New Zealand conditions, nothing of its laws. She was the stranger here. She had no claim on the estate. All she had was the bundle of traveler's checks in her bag and the draft of the small nest egg that had come to her from the sale of the cottage after the mortgage had been paid and their air fares. It would have to do till she got things settled and she found some sort of job. But where?

They picked up the children, full of excited chatter. Euan Hazeldean stopped in town, taking in thermos bottles, emerging with them full, and with a box that looked like sandwiches and cake.

"We'll have our tea on the way, in a picnic spot called Mount Stuart," he announced.

He turned right at the Octagon, headed up Stuart Street to Highgate, where they could look down on the whole city with its spires and University buildings, ships at anchor, countless bays and headlands. To the west stretched range upon range of gray blue mountains, folding into each other and losing themselves in the horizon.

Callum remarked on these. Euan Hazeldean laughed. "Just pimples, really. Our big stuff is farther back. We head toward them but don't reach them, though some day I'll take you youngsters up to Wakatipu, a big lake, snow fed. We run south about forty miles now, then go about seventy-odd miles west."

Lindsay noticed he'd said he'd take the youngsters. Not her. He was going to accept the children as family, but she would remain the cuckoo in the nest, the one with no claim. Yet surely Lex Bairdmore owed her something too? She had helped to rear his children and they still needed her to care for them.

She was driven into the unknown with a man so hard in nature that he had no condemnation for his employer, who had deserted a woman when she had needed him most. A farmer needs a wife who can pull her weight, was all he had said. No 'in sickness and in health' about that! Did this country breed men like that, then? Men you could not trust or admire. She would feel her way, hold a watching brief for the children. There was something here not aboveboard.

Yet it was a beautiful country. They dipped down to the Kaikorai Valley, full of new houses, wooden and brick, mostly gaily painted, past a woollen mill and a most modern high school in a gem of a setting, with a burn — or did they call them creeks here — purling through emerald turf, a verdant hillside splashed with the gold of gorse above it.

This had been a rutted side road not long ago, between the mill and the abattoirs, but now it was part of a great new highway, designed to bypass the city traffic. Remnants of former rusticity showed in farmlets above the suburban houses and a crooked sign that said Mulberry Lane.

At the Main South Road they turned right, and below them on the driver's side lay the Taieri Plain stretching to the Maungatuas and the gorges.

"And this is November," marveled Lindsay, looking at the hawthorn hedges sweet in ivory and rose, the fat lambs gamboling on rolling hills, lilac, clematis, laburnum clothing the farm gardens with scented loveliness, rhododendrons, azaleas and camellias splashing color everywhere, roses, the first of the season, nodding from the fences.

"Oh, a mountain ash!" she said nostalgically, as by the side of the road they passed rowan trees clotted with cream blossom. "There are so many of our trees here — I didn't realize there would be. There's a chestnut with all its candles out — and those are sycamores and oaks, surely?"

"Yes, and we have our larch woods and fir plantations, pines and poplars and willows. They all do extremely well here."

This was better, they were getting on

to an easier footing.

"I was expecting to see more native bush, evergreen stuff," she told him.

"You'll see it further back in the hills, in pockets in the gullies. Most of it round here is English, planted by the pioneers. I'm afraid a lot of the original bush was burned off to create pastureland." He slowed down. "See that hillside there — those are *kowhais*, similar to, but not quite as pretty as, laburnums. Their flowering is just over, but it's a lovely sight to see our honey-eating birds dipping into their bells. They turn upside down to do it."

Callum said, "You mean the *tuis* and bell birds? The ones with the brush on their tongues?"

"Yes, and the wax-eyes or silver-eyes, which are really Australian. One Maori name for them is *Kanohimopwhiti*, which means spectacle eye and is an excellent description. I can see you didn't waste your time at the museum. Good show."

"Oh, we knew all that before we arrived, didn't we, Morag? Lindsay said if we were about to become New Zealanders we'd better know a bit about

64

the country, so she got us some books from the library."

In the car mirror Euan Hazeldean's eyes met hers. "So you intend to stay, do you?"

"Yes, I feel the children should be in their father's home, put down roots."

He said nothing to that, merely pointed out a signpost that said Berwick. "You'll find a good many Scots names, Bannockburn, Ettrick, Roxburgh, Teviot and so on. There's quite a happy intermingling of Scots and Maori names, just as there is of European and native trees. That's as it should be, growing side by side. And in the main there is just as happy a mingling of Maori and *Pakeha. Pakeha* means white man."

Lindsay liked his views on that and was resentful that she did. It would make the situation must less complicated if she completely and utterly disliked this man, found no good in him. Because remembered distrust was in her heart. Because of Lex Bairdmore's charm, because of Robin Lockhart's charm. Something that could add up to disillusionment and tragedy.

At Milton, in the Bruce County, they turned west into yellowed rolling hills. They stopped at Mount Stuart, climbed over a rickety gate, went through English trees into a glade where a river flowed, a place of green translucent light and a mosaic of sun and shadow through the great branches. They spread out their picnic tea on a huge stump. Euan Hazeldean poured hot tea, produced lemonade for the children, opened the box of delectable savories and sandwiches. It was surprising how hungry they were.

Morag tossed back her tawny elfin locks. "Please, Mr. Hazeldean, may we cross the burn on that fallen log and explore the other side for a wee bittie?"

"Sure . . . as long as you don't get wet. It's quite shallow and safe. Better do it barefoot, though. Off you go."

Lindsay moved nervously. "We — we don't want to delay you. You may have things to attend to at the farm, milking and so on. Don't let the children make nuisances of themselves."

He shook his head. "We're only milking three, and by machine. My man will attend to it with Neill's help."

He called to the children, "Take the first fork on the track to the left, it'll bring you uphill to a good view." He turned to her. "I imagine the children will appreciate not being bustled, rushed across the world as they have been."

Lindsay said stiffly, "I couldn't help that. My stepfather asked to see them. He suggested coming by air and as soon as possible. Although he said he'd probably have a year, I couldn't delay in case. There were no sea passages for eighteen months, except for Kiwis returning home. And — I would have liked to have had him see the children before he died.

He was facing her across the tree stump and screwing flask tops on. His look was sardonic.

"Yes, you could have tied up this legacy, too, then, of course."

If Lindsay flinched, it was inwardly. Her eyes held his. "If that's what you want to think, think it. I had no need to hurry for that reason. My stepfather said he was leaving me a legacy. I naturally assumed it to be signed and sealed — with that will. Well, it wasn't. As long as the children have enough for their wants, that will do me. I've enough to keep myself meanwhile. I can earn my own keep, if that's what's worrying you."

"How? We're fifteen miles from the nearest township."

"I'm a trained farmhand. No doubt I can make myself useful enough at Rhoslochan to earn my board, and I don't want more than that."

His laugh got her on the raw. "A farmhand! A fat lot of good on a New Zealand farm. It's a bit different. We don't winter any stock inside, even in the far south. They spend all year outside, with a bit of feeding out. And on Rhoslochan we do very little cropping. Not as you would know it, anyway. It's a sheep run purely and simply. Milk just for ourselves and the married couple. And for orphaned lambs, of course. But you've forgotten something, in any case. You can't stay — long — at Rhoslochan."

Lindsay swallowed. "Rhoslochan is the children's home, their father's home. They have a right to be there. And where they are, I stay. I won't turn you out of your no doubt comfortable quarters, Mr. Hazeldean, *I'll* take the *whare*."

He laughed mirthlessly. "I can just imagine your martyred airs. We pride ourselves that we dispense a Scots brand of hospitality here . . . Yes, laugh, Miss Macrae. You and Morag will have the spare room. It had been prepared for Mr. Macrae and Callum. And Callum can have the sun porch I'd allotted to Morag. He could bunk with Neill, but Neill's used to a room of his own, and besides, he studies late. It's his School Cert year. *I'll* have the *whare*."

"And *I'll* put up with *your* martyred airs, I suppose." She hurriedly changed the subject as she saw his black look. "Will — will Neill, too, resent our coming? The children are looking forward to meeting him. I wouldn't like them to get a set back. I — "

"Neill was only sorry he couldn't come to Dunedin to meet them. You may find me lacking in romance, Miss Macrae, but not Neill. He's a born romantic, thinks it's like a novel to have some family suddenly turn up — a long-lost brother and sister."

Lindsay blinked. "When did I say you were unromantic?"

"Coming down the stairs from the lawyer's. Let me prod your memory. You couldn't imagine any woman sitting by the tide weeping for this Jock o' Hazeldean!"

Lindsay reddened. "I didn't say just that, I only — "

"You only implied it. Full of evasions, aren't you? I like direct speech, myself."

Lindsay's chin jerked up. "I find that amusing . . . from *you*!"

The brows came down. "Just what do you mean by that? I don't think I care to have my straightforwardness questioned."

"I can well imagine that. Makes you uneasy, does it?"

His eyes narrowed to slits. "Explain that, please!"

"I've no intention of explaining it at this stage. But you should realize I'm here to protect the children's interests. And if I'm not satisfied about things and the way they've been done I shall — Oh, Morag, not *that* branch! Back on to the other one, quick! Oh, save and keep us,

70

look what she's done now!"

Euan Hazeldean beat her to the stream by two strides, splashed in, hauled Morag out. She had been in no danger, it was very shallow, with a shingle bed, but being Morag she was still thoroughly drenched.

Lindsay was furious. Hazeldean had found them enough of a nuisance without this.

She turned round on him, forestalling his reprimand, "But it's your fault anyway! I never let either of them go near water unless they're dressed for it. And if we're delayed it serves you right!"

Callum and Morag looked dismayed. Morag's lips trembled.

"L-Lindsay? You don't usually get in such a stramashing about a wee thing like falling in the burrn!"

Morag's Scots accent was always stressed when she was upset.

Unexpectedly, Euan Hazeldean intervened as peacemaker.

"No, and she wouldn't now, but for the fact that your sister's tired after all this flying from Scotland. It took far more out of her than you kids. She had all the responsibility. That's why she lost her temper. But it doesn't matter two hoots. Callum, back to the car — here's the key — and get your sister's bag and bring it here as fast as you can." He shouted after him, "There's a big dust cloth in the left side pocket. Bring it to use as a towel."

He took out a huge handkerchief, wiped Morag's face. He started to chuckle. "You sure did make a good job of it, didn't you poppet!" He took her hair, squeezed the ends gently, began rubbing it.

Lindsay reached over to take on the job. He waved her away, went on rubbing. Once more Morag beamed at him. Lindsay felt a queer sensation. It couldn't be jealousy, could it? It would only be natural if Morag was drawn to him. He had interfered to save her a scolding. And there had never been a man in the family in all Morag's little life.

Callum came back with the bag. Lindsay retired behind a big willow with Morag, rubbed so vigorously that the child protested, then garbed her in a warm green sweater and Black Watch trousers. When she picked up the hairbrush Morag snatched it off her, ran away, came up to Hazeldean, and said appealingly, "You brush it, won't you? Lindsay's in the mood to tug."

Smiling, Euan Hazeldean began to brush, then comb, most gently. Lindsay couldn't remember when she had felt so cross. He was going to undermine her influence with the children. Was this all part of a plan to shut her out of the family circle? Come to that, how dare he! He was only the farm manager, wasn't he?

She gave no hint of her chagrin. She just shrugged, laughed, and finished packing the picnic things, pushing Morag's wet clothing into a plastic bag, then went across and said in a normal tone, "Better let me tie it into a ponytail, Magsie, that'll keep the damp hair off your shoulders."

Morag submitted.

They headed into the Manuka Gorge and realized that here indeed was pure New Zealand.

"An ice trap in winter," said Hazeldean.

They came out of the dark gorge, *manuka*-clad, into rolling country again.

"Grand hills for sheep," commented Lindsay.

Hazeldean smiled. "Very apt. There was a prize winning novel for the Otago centenary in 1948 called just that. It was written of this part of the country too. Waitahuna actually, I believe."

"Waitahuna?" repeated Callum. "Wasn't that where Gabriel Read first found gold in — um — 1861?"

"A wee bit farther on — Lawrence, but as near as makes no difference. Waitahuna is part of the goldmining district. It put Otago on the map of the world. Good lad, you've retained what your sister insisted you read. I'll run you up to Gabriel's Gully, to the very spot. It's just a short distance."

Lindsay decided he was making up to the children. A cold fear clutched her heart. Would he try to separate them from her? What if later, underlining his guardianship, he forced her to earn her living in the nearest township, and keep the children at the homestead?

The former mining towns still had

74

derelict pubs close together that had served the miners, but many of them were now being transformed into modern business premises in the small towns, or pulled down as eyesores. They could see everywhere in contours and gashes the evidences of how man, in feverish search for quick wealth, had changed the landscape.

Lawrence dreamed beneath its trees and hills. It was hard not to imagine the jostling, lawless crowds, the bawdy songs coming from the saloons, the dark and treacherous deeds of those days, the sheer valour and endurance of the gold-hungry men.

They turned along a shingled road that was scarcely more than a track, came to the pick and shovel monument and gazed at a tiny burn coursing gently along, tried to imagine what it must have been like a hundred years ago, with this gully alive with men.

Euan Hazeldean looked around him. "Nature covered up the worst scars with living green. You'd never think that every inch of this ground has been dug over, torn apart, not once but many times, sluiced and washed. Well, we'd better be going."

Lindsay was glad the children asked so many questions. She was dying to ask them herself, but didn't want to appear eager to become friendly.

She had to admit he answered them all good-humoredly. Yes, they were cabbage trees. Ugly, tufty things, weren't they? No, no a palm, he believed they belonged to the lily family, something you couldn't believe till the heads were in bloom and the whole countryside was enveloped in glorious perfume. Neill had a very tall one he used as a lookout. He had nine-inch nails driven in for steps all the way. Yes, sure he'd let them use it.

The blue gums were Australian. They shed their bark instead of their leaves, and were aromatic and beautiful. You couldn't now imagine New Zealand without them. The tangled thorn were *matagouri*, or wild Irishman as the settlers had dubbed them. Yes, they did look like something out of the desert.

Not many wild flowers, a few foxgloves, borage, Californian poppy, buttercups, daisies, clover, lupin and broom. Most of

76

the native wild flowers were delicate and pale in color, but *rata* and native mistletoe were both vivid scarlet creepers.

Yes, that was watercress in the streams there, but you don't eat it here, too much danger of getting hydatids from the dogs — they were getting it under now, though, with compulsory dosing and insisting that the farmers didn't feed the dogs raw offal. So make sure you scour your hands — don't just run 'em under the tap — if you've been handling the dogs.

Sheep farms gave way to fruit farms, nestled in under mountains, that here and there still pocketed snow in gullies and ridges, blindingly white with the westering sun on them.

The mighty Clutha river cut like a peacock blue green ribbon through the brown bare hills below the road, forcing its mighty channel of snow water, drained from two huge lakes, Wakatipu and Wanaka, into foaming splendor, on its way to the Pacific.

At Roxburgh he stopped to let them see the blue water of the dam behind the Hydro and watch it coming down the spillway like a giant's soapsuds forced from a mammoth wringer — which was Morag's idea. They passed the fruit factory, the huge sheds where fruit and berries were packed before being airlifted to the markets of Auckland in the subtropical north, sped on through and around great bluffs, saw ruins of old sod cottages and deserted accommodation houses where the gold coaches, under escort, had put up for the night; saw a monument marking the spot where miners, lost in the trackless hills of the last century, had perished in a blizzard.

Beyond them glittered snowpeaks, clustering, Euan Hazeldean told them, around fathomless lakes miles away. Lindsay thought with an ache in her heart she did not understand, *Why, I could love this land, given a chance, given a welcome*. It was Scotland on a bigger, more rugged scale. A challenging, primitive terrain. What an air of space about it, how few and far between the farms.

It was getting still more and more rugged. "Although we don't go as far as Alexandra, quite, where the outcrops of schist rock are quite fantastic. The weather has beaten them into shapes out of phantasmagoria. Alexandra is like an oasis of cool waters and green trees with above it the barren rocks of Aden. It sizzles in summer, the sun striking back from the rock walls surrounding it."

They turned a bend. He waved a hand at the left of the road. "Rhoslochan land starts from here."

"And ends where?" It was Callum who asked.

"You can't see where it ends — it goes right to the next bluff, round a couple more corners. And its boundary behind the house can't be seen either. Goes back a couple of miles behind the hills."

Lindsay thought dazedly, *Then do they reckon farms in miles, not acres?*

Aloud she said, somewhat tartly, "Well, there certainly ought to be enough room for us all without fighting."

Euan Hazeldean said quietly, "We won't be needing to fight."

Lindsay thought it sounded as if he fondly imagined he would get all his own way!

3

THEY swept in over cattle stops between an avenue of poplars that would be a glory in autumn but now were a wall of solid green. It was lush and fertile and apparently cultivated well up the hills into which the rolling land merged, till the vivid emerald of the sown pastures met the yellow of tussock and the barren outcrops of jagged, pancakelike formations of schist.

On the left was a paddock that looked almost scythed and was planted around its immense acreage with English trees till it looked like a park. A more closely shaven strip could be a cricket pitch.

The manager said to the children, waving a hand, "We call it the Sunday-school picnic paddock." It sounded disarming. Was it a case of outward respectability cloaked questionable practices . . . a juggling with the estate funds, something that wouldn't bear looking into?

On the right, in a green-bushed gully,

was the silver gleam of a brook that reached the farmland to thread its way among willows till it went out of sight. Still no glimpse of a house.

They turned a shoulder of hill, saw trees clustered about outbuildings, and there, above rocky terraces, naturally formed, its gleaming white face to the sun, was Rhoslochan. Its roof was corrugated iron newly painted green, its wooden pillars were hung with bloomy boughs of wistaria, a cascade of shot silk roses, pink and full blown, hung from a rose arch. Virginia creeper in green leaf clung lovingly to the brick chimney.

Peony roses lit up the corners of the garden, delphiniums had fat buds, still tight, ranunculas and anemones rioted in crimsons and purples, alyssum in lavender and white frothed at the weedy edges of the lawn.

It was a garden that had been loved once but had been neglected of late. Had Lex been the gardener till he was taken ill? Probably all Hazeldean and Neill had time for was to mow the lawns. Her heart lifted a little. Maybe they would allow her to tend the garden. Or were they harsh creatures, with little patience for frills, preferring their time and the time of others to be spent on money-yielding projects?

The driveway curved around to the back, followed through pines and gum trees, and they stopped at the entrance to the kitchen garden, well stocked but choked with weeds.

There was a clatter from one of the sheds, a clang as a can was dropped and out shot a youthful figure, all eagerness. It was wearing jeans, had black hair that fell forward, blue eyes and a well-cut mouth, was long and lean and the face had a good jawline.

Lindsay stared in amazement. The figure stopped in its headlong rush and stared at Callum, standing by the rear door.

They all looked transfixed, except Euan Hazeldean, who was grinning as if he had expected just this. They looked from one to the other of the boys, then Neill spoke dazedly.

"Well, what d'you know?" he demanded. "What d'you know? Imagine meeting your double . . . two sizes smaller!"

Callum smiled his slow smile, held out his hand, "Och, Neill, now I can really realize I've a brother."

Neill gripped his hand, relinquished it, then said, "And this is Morag, my sister! But not a bit like dad."

"Isn't she?" asked Euan Hazeldean. "Wait a bit, Neill." He stepped behind Morag, gently pulled back the straying elfin locks that had long since escaped their ponytail and tucked them behind Morag's ears. "See . . . your father's own pointed ears . . . the one feature you and Callum didn't inherit."

Lindsay said quickly, too quickly, "But Morag is like my mother." Immediately she wished it unsaid, it sounded grudging, jealous.

But Neill said quickly, holding out a hand to Lindsay in a way that reminded her of Lex's easy charm, "Well, it looks as if I've got myself two sisters, not one. I was just about bowled over when Mr. MacWilson gave me your message, Euan, that Lindsay Macrae was a girl. Euan, I've got the table set but I didn't know what to do about swapping the beds around. Wynne came down and started the meal, but she wasn't too well and went home. I think it's pretty near."

"Do you mean she's exhausted because it's near her time, or has she actually started the baby?"

"I wouldn't know. She probably thinks I'm too young to be told details. Anyway she went over to the bungalow, and I went across to the shed and told Mick I'd finish the milking if he went across to her."

"Good lad. I'll give them a call and find out how she is. Come on in, everybody."

The house was one of the older homesteads, beautifully preserved outside but showing lack of a woman's constant care inside. Everything needed polishing or scrubbing, though it had a mellow, homely air. Nothing here that a week or two's concentrated effort wouldn't restore. Lindsay's spirits rose. She could make herself useful here.

Euan Hazeldean said, "As a rule, we're more spick-and-span than this, but with Wynne's time so near she couldn't give us more than a day a week and we've had to shift for ourselves, and it's a busy time outside. Of course, once the baby comes we can't expect her at all."

Lindsay said hesitatingly, because the term vulture still rankled, "Perhaps that's where I could help."

He was curt and watchful, as if he felt her to be insincere.

"If you want to. Bit different from what you expected, isn't it? No domestic help, no real signs of wealth."

Lindsay lifted her chin. "I'm not entirely ignorant about New Zealand. I know that it's rare to employ domestics here. But I would say — " she swept around and looked about her " — that till fairly recently this was quite well looked after. Was there a housekeeper before this?"

Even as she said it she knew a moment of dread. Had her stepfather had some woman living here? Remembering his facile charm it was quite likely, and Lindsay did not want to create embarrassment for Neill's sake.

The manager said quite easily, "Oh, yes. My mother. She looked after Neill for years. I came here as a young man. But my mother is away looking after

my sister, will be for some time yet
. . . perhaps another six months." He
suddenly chuckled. "My sister, believe
it or not, suddenly presented the family
with triplets! A great girl for overdoing
things, our Bess. She's always been a
goer. But it's an all-day job feeding and
bathing and dressing three. And there are
two older children."

His mother had kept house here! The
sort of job women liked. No other women
in the family. Certainly these Hazeldeans
had dug themselves in. No wonder they
were wary of strangers coming in to assess
the situation. And Neill was so young, so
vulnerable, so alone . . . till now. Lindsay
felt a wave of protectiveness sweep over
her, for Neill. If she found out just what
was going on she could help him too, of
course.

Euan Hazeldean picked up her bag,
gestured toward the stairs. They were
luxuriously carpeted, but the banisters
were thick with dust. Lindsay itched to
get at it.

They could hear Neill and Callum
talking nineteen to the dozen.

The manager pushed open a door

with his foot, gestured her in. It was beautifully furnished, and guests must often have been entertained. Each headboard contained a shelf of light reading, had a good lamp above. There was a towel rack, two chintz-covered easy chairs in the windows that were open to the evening breeze. Some preparation had been made here, for the candlewick bedspreads were freshly laundered, the beds turned down.

"This was for Callum and a male guardian, of course," said Hazeldean. "I believe Wynne prettied up the sunporch for Morag — so I'll get Neill to remove the doll Wynne put there for her, and the little-girl-type books."

Lindsay went straight across to the open windows where wistaria nodded in, and caught her breath at the loveliness outside.

There it lay behind the house, not visible from the road, a tiny lochan fed from the watershed of the hills about it, stained as pink as the shot silk rosed by the setting sun.

"How absolutely enchanting!" she cried, forgetting enmity. "I didn't dream there actually was a lake. I thought it would be just named for some place in Scotland . . . Rhoslochan, the little pink lake. What a gem!"

"Yes," said Jock of Hazeldean's voice at her shoulder, "any wonder I — any wonder we — love the place?"

Lindsay swung around, looked at him. "Mr. Hazeldean, there's a lot I don't understand. *I'm* not setting up any claim to this place — I've no right to it whatever. But the children have, just as Neill has. I haven't even any say in its running. You're acting as if I wanted to take charge, to engage another manager or something. I can't understand your reactions. I'm simply here to look after my half brother and sister. I know I'm a complication at the moment with no other woman in the house. I'm sorry about you having to sleep in the hut — I've offered to do that myself, but you won't let me — but if you're prepared to meet me halfway I'm sure we'll find a way out of our difficulties.

"Let's go down and get our meal, get the children settled, and we'll try to intrude as little as possible on you.

I think it's a great pity you aren't married and that there isn't, in any case, a manager's house on the estate."

"I think you'd better know," he said, his face dark, "that I stay here, in possesion of the house."

"Meaning that that is in your contract?"

"Meaning just that. If you have any doubts on the matter you can ask Jim MacWilson."

"Very well. But I suggest we leave all that sort of thing for a couple of days or so to allow me to get my bearings. I have to be with the children, and this happens to be their home."

But would they ever feel at home anywhere again? Lindsay thought despairingly. She followed him down the stairs. Could it be that he was going to make things so uncomfortable for her here that, of her own accord, she would move out? If that was so, it meant only one thing, that the affairs of the estate needed someone on the spot, to look into them.

The children eased the situation. The three of them were heartwarmingly pleased with themselves and their new relationship. The fact that Lindsay and

Hazeldean hardly spoke to each other went unnoticed in the general chatter.

Lindsay marveled at their adaptability, their calm acceptance of the situation. It was simply, to them, a romantic happening. They had found a new brother, this was their home. What fun!

Neill had set the table in the dining room and, knowing he couldn't attempt flowers, had placed a bowl of fruit as a centerpiece. It was a long table with a snowy cloth that probably hadn't been used since Mrs. Hazeldean went north. The silver was good but in need of polishing, the food plain, but attractive.

Neill said, "I'm not very good at shredding lettuce, so I just washed it."

Lindsay thought he'd managed well and said so. There was a dish of hard-boiled eggs, one of radishes, tomatoes and a jug of mayonnaise dressing that was so smooth and creamy that this Wynne must have made it, as well as the scones set in a basket lined with a napkin. There was honey in the comb, a huge slab of cheese, a cold leg of mutton. Euan Hazeldean himself made the tea and poured it.

After the meal Lindsay stood up, pushed her chair back and said in an undertone to the manager — under cover of some wrangle that had developed between the three children on the relative and average sizes of Scottish salmon and New Zealand salmon — "I would very much like to help with the household chores. I'll do so if you won't think I'm taking to much upon myself. That way I would at least feel I did something toward earning my keep."

His dark countenance was unreadable. "Fair enough. When you want help don't be too stiff-necked to ask for it. These past few months we've had to fend for ourselves, so we're used to it."

Lindsay took this stricture with no outward sign that her hackles rose at his assumption. She ran upstairs, changed her blue tweed jacket for a cardigan, donned a sensible apron. She wanted no supercilious looks from that dark-avised man downstairs over frilly aprons.

She called the twins. "We'll have to get the dishes over before you go exploring — besides, there's plenty of time ahead to get acquainted with the place." She looked up to see that dark gaze upon her and colored to the roots of her light brown hair.

Did he think to freeze them out soon? Did he regard them as birds of passage, innocents who might be expected to accept a lump sum and go back to Scotland? Not if she knew it!

She said to Neill, "You'll want to study, I suppose, Neill, if you're taking exams at present. And this has been disrupting."

Euan Hazeldean cut in. "No, Neill is one who doesn't leave it all to the last. I always think the knowledge should be acquired before the exams start and I like Neill to relax in between the exam sessions." He grinned at Neill. "It's not every night a boy acquires a new brother and sister! Off you go with them and show them round. I'll do the wiping up. Off you go, all of you."

The three disappeared instantly with the unspoken but kindred thought that it was best not to linger where grownups were concerned in case of mind changing.

Morag's voice floated back to them.

"Good guy, isn't he, Neill?"

"Somebody likes me, anyway," said that hatefully derisive voice in Lindsay's ear as she vigorously swished dishes out of the soapy water.

She resisted the temptation to point out that children were given to make rapid, often unreliable judgments, that first impressions were often false. She wanted to say bitterly that no one would have thought her stepfather anything but charming.

She said instead, "I notice Neill calls you Euan. I thought you said everyone made it Jock."

"Everybody bar family," he said nonchalantly.

Unseen, she pursed her lips. So. Considered himself family, did he? No wonder — with his mother and himself ensconced in a modestly luxurious home, probably enjoying all sorts of unorthodox prerequisites. With his employer gone no doubt this Euan Hazeldine hoped to feather his own nest. There would be no one to account to, and probably Jim MacWilson knew little about farming. No wonder he didn't want anyone here who did know farming, even if he affected to despise farm girls from the other side of the world.

She said stiffly as she mopped up the gleaming laminex bench, "I hope you won't think me curious if I peer into the cupboards. I just want to familiarize myself with the contents so I can cook breakfast fairly speedily and efficiently."

"Oh, don't bother, we're used to rustling it up for ourselves."

"That's hardly necessary with a woman in the house. I'd have to get ours, in any case. I feel sufficient of a cuckoo in the nest without you having to feed us. What time do you get up?"

"That's it. Five-thirty. Too early."

"Not for me. Last summer I had to be up at quarter to five to get our chores done and the breakfast ready for the youngsters to heat up and lunches cut before I was due at the farm. After mother died, I mean."

He relented a little. "I don't breakfast then. I have a cup of tea and a snack, then come and cook breakfast at seven. Otherwise it's too early for Neill. He leaves at eight on the school bus."

"Does that take only the high school children, or will Callum and Morag be able to use it too when they start?"

"They will use it too, but they won't go as far as Alexandra. Their school is nearer, a little two-teacher one at Crannog."

"Crannog? A Gaelic name? Let me see . . . a lake dwelling?"

"Yes. Though I didn't know it meant that. There's a wee lochan nearby. It's all fenced in and used as a swimming pool for the youngsters. Other schools that have to raise the money for their learners' training pools are green with envy when they see Crannog. It's as safe as can be, too. And grand as a skating rink in winter. I'll make arrangements for them to start Monday."

She dared not resent that. 'I'll make arrangements.' It was going to be hard to realize that she was not the twins' sole guardian now. It was just like Lex Bairdmore to appoint someone so utterly hostile, someone whom she could not trust.

She dried her hands. "Now I'll make up your bed in this *whare*," she said.

"I'll do that."

"I much prefer to take on any extra work we've made."

He sighed. "I asked you not to be stiff-necked with pride."

Lindsay set her lips, opened a cupboard, took out linen.

"It's rather tiresome to be accredited with motives that don't exist, Mr. Hazeldean. Will the mattress be aired?"

"No. Hasn't been used for ages. But I'll take over my own mattress — an electrically heated one. We get record frosts here when there's snow on the mountains, and all the mattresses in the house are that kind."

"How odd," she mused.

"What's odd?"

"I took you for the Spartan type, who'd spurn too much comfort, think it beneath you, prefer to be tough."

His voice held a warning note. "I *can* be tough. Better not try me too far, Miss Macrae. I merely meant, since you're so touchingly concerned for my comfort, that my own mattress, by virtue of its being an electric one, is always aired. It can't harbor any dampness like kapok.

I wasn't intending to switch it on on a night like this. I'll show you the *whare* — there are three of them."

They were old army huts, barely but adequately furnished. They had little Dover stoves for heating. Lindsay supposed that when they had been used for single men they made their late cup of tea on that. The floor was covered with linoleum, there was a shabby bed, a corner wardrobe, a chest of drawers, a cupboard, a bedside light and a chair. A sheepskin served as a bedside rug.

Lindsay's expression was rueful. "I've complicated matters all right! Sorry to be turning you out of your room at the homestead, Mr. Hazeldean."

He laughed easily enough. "Nothing wrong with this. You ought to have seen some of the places I've slept in. I was shepherding for a couple of years in the high country. A lot of young chaps do. Very remote, nothing to spend your money on, and the best way to save for your own place I can think of. This will do for a day or two till we get something worked out. Maybe the — er — the estate could rent you a modest cottage in Alexandra, handy to school and not so isolated for you. It wouldn't be palatial, of course."

He looked at her sharply.

She thought he was looking for a fight, so she said quietly, "A very good idea."

It looked as if he did not want her here, apart from the conventions. Was he afraid she would notice things he did not want noticed?

They came out to find the afterglow gone and clouds settling on the hilltops so close above them. The last sleepy twittering of the birds was dying down into the darkening twilight. It sounded like home. Most of the birds were English birds, she had already noticed. Suddenly she pricked her ears.

"Was that an owl I heard?"

"Yes. The morepork. Its Maori name is the *ruru*. It calls 'More pork,' all the time."

They could hear the happy voices of the children down at the lochan.

"They'll be quite safe with Neill," he told her. "He's most reliable, a great boy for taking responsibility."

"In that respect, then," said Lindsay,

"he doesn't take after his father."

After a moment of silence Hazeldean said slowly and deliberately, "Miss Macrae, I think it would be better if we did not discuss Lex Bairdmore. I think Neill would be hurt if he heard you to refer to his father like that. Possibly the other children hold no great opinion of him, so I hope they keep their own counsel. But I insist you don't speak disparagingly of Lex."

Their eyes met, his dark and inscrutable, Lindsay's gray and cold.

"The children have never heard one word of criticism of their father from either my mother or myself." She walked into the house with back stiff, a slim slip of a girl with light brown hair twisted up into a roll at the back of her head, and despite her slenderness, there was more than a hint of indomitableness in her walk.

Fortunately she was so physically exhausted that she fell asleep far sooner than she had dreamed she would.

★ ★ ★

She had her traveling clock set at the alarm, and as nothing was known to disturb Morag short of dragging her out of her bed, she wasn't worried about disturbing her. She was determined to beat Euan Hazeldean to it.

She slipped along to the bathroom quietly, had a quick wash so she wouldn't be accused of holding the manager up if he wanted to use it, dressed and slipped downstairs.

Thank goodness there was also an electric stove, so she didn't need to struggle with an unfamiliar fuel one yet. Maybe when Euan Hazeldean came in to find his cup of tea all ready he'd realize it might be handy to have her here. And he wouldn't need to break off his farm work to cook breakfast.

The sleeping arrangements were awkward, of course, but possibly that could be solved by putting a stretcher into one of the *whares* and having Morag sleep there with her. Her thoughts halted. *If* that thrawn and dour New Zealander would allow them. He was just the sort to stay there himself and enjoy a grievance!

She had peeped into his bedroom the night before, when passing, and found it almost luxurious. He might work it out that if he stayed in the hut, she would have to move to Alexandra soon for very shame's sake.

Lindsay grinned at herself in the mirror. Hazeldean just didn't know her, that was all! The Lindsays motto was Endure With Strength and the Macraes' was With Fortitude. She was going to see this thing out.

She tied back her hair simply in a ponytail and decided against jeans. He might think she wanted to work outside if she wore them. She slipped into a pale blue linen blouse with the sleeves pushed up and a bright peasant skirt.

She switched on the electric kettle and sliced up some brown bread and butter. He came in, looked at her, said sharply, "This wasn't necessary — I told you. I could get my own."

She was nonchalant. "Oh, I couldn't sleep. I'm not used to sleeping late, you see, so I thought I might as well save you the time. I hope you aren't the type to cut off your nose to spite your face.

The bathroom's free if you want it."

He looked at her and pulled a face. "I don't need the bathroom. I showered in the laundry. There's an extra shower room off it. And I'm not stupid, only strongminded. This is very nice. I'll call Mick. He's not used to looking after himself. Perhaps you could manage breakfast for him, too, later."

Lindsay's sense of humor made her want to grin back. His graciousness had spiked her guns nicely. She resisted the temptation.

Mick came in, looking pleased. He smiled at Lindsay. "Jolly good thing you turned out a woman, especially when Wynne's not on deck."

Lindsay smiled back, knew a lift of the heart. "Have you heard from the nursing home? How is — "

"Oh yes, last night. I took the children in to Wynne's cousin in Clyde — beyond Alex — and called back at the nursing home to find we had a wee daughter at last. Talk about quick! Wynne was in seventh heaven and extremely well, thank goodness. I'm always terrified she'll have the bad time she did with the first. I told

102

her not to have any ideas about trying for a sister for her. Four is quite enough, my nerves won't stand more! I was so pleased with myself that I went a mile past the cattle stops before I realized I was heading for Roxburgh. I've always wanted a daughter to take to football matches."

They both gaped.

"What an extraordinary things to say," said Lindsay. "I would have thought a man with three little boys would — "

"Oh, I've always thought it looked good to see a man at a football match with his daughter," said Mick ingenuously.

Euan Hazeldean's lips twitched. "Probably somebody else's daughter, Mick."

They all laughed.

Mick turned to Lindsay. "You realize that when we say football here we mean rugby? Association football is merely soccer."

"An odd distinction," said Lindsay lightly, "when you think that rugby is largely a matter of hugging the ball like a grizzly bear."

Mick blinked. "Heavens, Jock, we'll

never take her to a test match at Carisbrooke . . . she'd get lynched in the first five minutes!"

Lindsay relented. "I like watching rugby," she admitted, "though I prefer foot — I prefer soccer. I've seen your All-Blacks play. But it'll be tough on Callum."

Euan Hazeldean said, "Oh, Neill plays soccer for his school. There's a junior team in town, too. Now Neill's got his license to drive, I shan't have to take him into practices and matches, so Callum will be able to go in with him on Saturdays."

Lindsay began to feel happier. Then he must be thinking that they would stay on.

A pity then that he went on to say, "Oh, I forgot, by winter you'll probably be in Alex."

Mick got the idea. "Yes, I suppose something like that will have to be arranged. Unless . . . won't your mother be back by then, Jock?"

"Possibly, but even next winter Elizabeth may need a good deal of help with those triplets. I can see mother flying up and down whenever she thinks Bess may need a rest or when they have measles or whooping cough or something. I think it would be best to settle Miss Macrae in town."

Mick got to his feet, pushed his cup back and said, grinning, "I reckon you'd better marry her, Jock. We could do with another woman on the place, especially an early-rising cook. You've been a bachelor long enough." They went out laughing.

Lindsay didn't laugh. *Marriage*. For *usefulness*. Och, she knew it was only banter, but weren't men unromantic! She realized by now that Robin, too, had probably assessed her qualities as a farmer's wife. Never mind. Perhaps at present her long acquaintance with hard work would serve her well. She looked round the kitchen and all her homemaking instincts rose to the fore.

It was a delightfully old-time kitchen, rather a surprise after the modern, wealthy-looking farmhouses they had passed yesterday. The window that caught a glimpse of the little lochan was bright with geraniums, the shady window by the entrance porch had ferns in it, brought from the bush, she supposed, but they had been neglected for some time. They were withered, set in soil like concrete. She filled an enamel jug and began watering them.

The lochan still had a pink tinge about it, in the crevices of the rocks that clustered about it. Neill had told her last night that it was wild thyme. It grew all over this part and people came from far and near to gather it in for the mixed herbs sales.

She looked doubtfully at the coal stove. Perhaps she'd find this a good time to try it out. It had to be done sometime. First she all she hunted down some blacklead brushes. It had been kept well, but neglected lately, like everything else. When she had finished, it gleamed black and silver.

Now what had Neill told her? 'Open up both dampers till she gets a start, then almost close them, but not too soon or she'll smoke.'

The trouble was, what was too soon? She soon found out. Smoke poured madly out, making her choke, and she had to rush around and open all the windows. Then she erred on the other side and the fire burned away, but in three-quarters of an hour it was purring gently and glowing red.

The morning was fresh enough for her to be glad of the warmth. Dew lay on paddock and hill. She must remember paddock and not field.

She started the breakfast preparation and went up to wake the children. She found Neill looking over some textbooks and notes.

"Neill, I hope our arrival wasn't too badly timed, and too distracting," Lindsay began.

Neill grinned, pushing back his hair in a gesture so much Callum's, Lindsay could hardly believe it. "Oh, it's geography today. My pet subject. Don't worry, Lindsay, last night didn't matter. Euan's such a slave driver on the matter of study that I was well ahead. I was just looking over. Are the kids up?"

"Almost . . . and raring to go. I'm glad your exams will be over by the weekend, Neill. You three should have a good time."

"Yes. They can both ride, can't they?

I'll take them over the boundaries — if you're nervous about them you can come, too. You could have Euan's mount, I can take dad's and we have a couple of ponies."

Lindsay said quickly, "Euan would have to offer it himself, Neill, before I could take it."

"He will, don't worry."

Lindsay went away wondering if that meant that Neill did count himself as the young master.

Hazeldean and Mick were quite appreciative of the breakfast and she hoped they were unaware of her nervousness lest it not be to their liking. Cooking was a chancy thing at any time, and on a new stove, conscious of the estate manager's antagonism, she wanted to prove herself.

But the porridge was as smooth as could be, the sausages evenly browned and the gravy all gravy should be, and giving them strict attention, there were no brown lace frills around the eggs.

Just as well no one knew she'd put four slices of toast in the hens' bucket before she got the pop-up toaster regulated to a rather dry loaf. She guessed they wouldn't get bread every day.

She told the children, after they had escorted Neill to the gates and waved the school bus off, that they might have an hour to explore, then she could do with their help inside.

"And for pity's sake, don't get into any mischief. Don't interfere with anything, don't leave any gates open, don't go near water. Oops! Sorry." She had cannoned into Hazeldean.

"Very negative!" he commented. "Psychologically speaking, it's better to be positive. Tell them what they *can* do."

She eyed him. "That's beautiful *theory*. After all, I know these children. I helped bring them up. If your psychology is no more sound than your ethics I'm not impressed, and I doubt if you're motivated by solicitude on the children's behalf . . . *I'd* think you'd want to put me in the wrong!"

Not only the children stared. Morag broke the silence. "I don't know what half those words mean!"

Hazeldean chuckled hatefully, "Neither does your sister, probably."

Morag wasn't satisfied. "But Lindsay sounded cross."

He chuckled again. "She was up too early. Needs more sleep. Makes some people liverish. Come on, Magsie, you too, Callum. I'll introduce you to the ponies, then you can ride around the sheep with me. Neill said you could ride and I could do with some help. Your sister will have mellowed by lunchtime, no doubt."

As they skipped off ahead of him, he turned and said over his shoulder, "Beat the gong at the door when it's ready. Twelve-thirty, please. Mick's spraying gorse in the paddock above his place."

Lindsay looked after their retreating backs and thought she'd rarely felt more furious . . . or felt furious more often. And how dare he use her pet name for Morag!

She went inside and began flinging the mats outside. She'd show him what a worker she was! That she wasn't just a money seeker but was prepared to earn her salt.

It was many moons since the kitchen at Rhoslochan had seen such activity.

Temper carried Lindsay on at a great pace. She'd never accomplished so much in so short a time.

Windows were cleaned, pictures taken down and dusted, corners swept of cobwebs, the curtains washed. They would dry soon enough, for the day was turning really hot, with a dry golden light washing over all, the sky an arc of palest blue.

The kitchen, despite its old-world air, had been modernized in the easier-work tradition, so it was mostly surface dirt, and with laminex table and benches and painted cupboards it soon gleamed spotlessly. She scrubbed the lemon and white linoleum tiles and then polished them till one could have eaten the proverbial meal off the floor. By the time she'd done that the curtains were dry enough to be ironed . . . they hung better slightly damp, anyway, and she put them back in their crisp black and white and daffodil checks at the two sets of windows that made it such a sunny place.

She even scrubbed the concrete-floored entry by hand, approving the steel

111

washbasin set in a corner, the racks for boots and the hooks for jackets.

At least when Wynne Sullivan came home with her baby she wouldn't have to face looking after two houses, and when Euan Hazeldean's mother came back it would not be to a backlog of work and a mighty spring cleaning.

Lindsay knew a moment of dread at the thought. No woman ever liked another taking over her domain, altering things round. She must be careful to make no radical changes. This was a home that had been loved and cosseted. You could tell that, even if at the moment it was tarnished and dusty.

Not that she was likely to be here when his mother came home. Euan Hazeldean wanted to install her in a cottage in Alexandra. He certainly didn't want her here. Was that a natural dislike of change, or that he didn't want her to notice things that wouldn't bear close scrutiny? Lindsay seized the brass polish.

Mick came in, calling out, "Thought there might be a cuppa on, Lindsay."

He added, smiling, as she picked up the singing kettle, "That okay with you, my calling you Lindsay? We go a fair bit on Christian names here, and it'd make you feel at home, wouldn't it?"

"I'd like it very much, Mick. I hope your wife will do the same."

Well, at least Mick can't know much about the situation, she thought.

He looked around appreciatively. "My word, what a difference. The boss will be thrilled. Great chap for his home. Oh, he joins in the community activities all right, but his real interests lie in his home."

In his home! Yes, there was no doubt whatever that the manager of Rhoslochan regarded it as his home. No wonder. He had worked here as a lad during his school holidays, as his mother was the housekeeper who'd looked after the small Neill. Now he resented the eruption of other heirs into the household.

It was natural, perhaps. It must have been a shock to hear that Lex Bairdmore had two children on the other side of the world . . . but justice had to be done. No, there must be more to it than that. Euan Hazeldean wanted absolute power. He wanted no questions asked. He and his mother were virtually kings of the castle.

Lindsay went upstairs. She did not go into the manager's bedroom. She stood on the threshold, looking in. It faced the distant mountains, one of the finest views in the whole house. It was easily as large as Lex Bairdmore's bedroom, next to it, and was certainly better furnished and more tastefully so. It was more like a bed-sitting room, three walls lined with well-filled bookcases, two deep armchairs, a standard lamp, a beautiful desk with a wall lamp above it.

She went into what was obviously Mrs. Hazeldean's room. It was a delightful one, fitted into the tower corner. The semicircular window in the tower was fitted with a curved window seat, padded with slightly faded chintz. There was a rosewood desk, a good piece, against the wall, an embroidery table, more bookcases, photographs of her son and daughter and her grandchildren, including the fascinating triplets.

The bedroom suite was a sturdy walnut one, possibly brought out in pioneer days. It looked rooted, belonging. For some reason it made Lindsay uneasy, unsure, as if it had always been Euan's mother's. That was ridiculous. She had been just the housekeeper.

She went into her room and Morag's, made the beds, put away their clothes, did the same in the porch Callum had occupied. Neill had made his bed, but the room was untidy. She left his books and notes as they were, sorted out some washing and took it downstairs. She couldn't tackle that till tomorrow. She found a lamb's-wool dustcloth and dusted the banisters. She mustn't work too long or attempt too much. The men would judge her most on her meals and she was more confident about her housework than her cooking.

There were chops in the fridge and tomatoes, too. That would do. There was a toaster, an infrared one, very similar to the one they had had in Scotland. At twelve-fifteen she banged the gong.

She knew once more the tremor of nervousness as she heard them coming to the house. She wasn't used to cooking for men. Had she done enough? Or miles too much? She hoped the butterflies in her stomach would soon subside. She hadn't really enjoyed a meal for days.

It was horrible to eat with a lump in your throat, apprehension tightening your stomach muscles. Suddenly she pulled herself together. "With Fortitude," she muttered to herself. "Remember you're a Macrae, Lindsay." Euan Hazeldean could not oust her. The will was fair enough, an equal share to each of Lex's children. He might easily have left the larger share to Neill, the first-born. She would have thought nothing of that. As the children's guardian she had to be with them. Hazeldean would realize that. But not their sole guardian, now. She must walk warily there. As far as the estate went he was only the manager. It was his new, personal relationship to the twins she feared.

They came in laughing and hungry. Morag and Callum wore expressions of sheer bliss. Lindsay felt a wave of love for them sweep over her. To have ponies of their own was something they had always longed for. All they'd had till now was the exercising of the ponies on the farm where Lindsay had worked.

"Mine is named Dapple Dee," said Morag, "and Callum's is Peggotty. Mine's gray, of course, and his black." She rubbed her seat. "I'm a wee bittie sore."

Euan Hazeldean looked every inch a son of the soil, the red brown column of his neck rising from a tartan shirt, his eyes crinkled at the corners, perhaps not laughter crow's-feet, Lindsay decided unjustly, but from screwing his eyes against the sun. He was always hatless.

He looked around the spotless kitchen. "Better go out and give your shoes an extra scrape, kids. Your sister has certainly been putting on the spit and polish."

As they went unquestioningly to do his bidding he said to her, as she turned from the stove, the pan of tomatoes in her hand, "Good idea . . . worked it all off, did you? When I feel that way I saw wood."

Lindsay did not bite, she merely said coldly, "You needn't make me out an ogre in the matter of dirty boots. After all, I *am* a farm girl. And while I like a clean house I don't like it that way at the expense of nagging everyone."

"Good for you," he said unrepentantly. "I can see that, in one respect at least,

117

you're a woman after my mother's own heart. I must write and tell her that her house is in good hands — she worries about it a bit."

Her house! Oh, yes, these Hazeldeans had certainly dug themselves in.

As she placed a dish of fried potatoes on the table, he caught her wrist, forcing her to look up at him.

His tone was dry. "You know, Miss Macrae, when a woman has looked after a house for years and years, mothering the son of the house, she *does* look upon it as her home."

Lindsay's cheeks flamed. "I didn't say — "

"You didn't need to. You have no poker face. You can't hide your feelings."

She looked him straight in the eye. "That's nothing to be ashamed of, Mr. Hazeldean. It makes for sincerity. I'm quite unable to read *your* expressions, I find." She shook off his hand. The children came in, Mick at their heels.

The meal proceeded quite amicably. When it was over Lindsay said, "You youngsters can skip the dishes if you like to go out and cut the lawns. Will that be all right by you, Mr. Hazeldean? Callum could mow and Morag could cut the edges."

"Sure thing. Callum, have you ever used a motor-mower?"

"Yes, a rotary one. I used one at home. I used to earn pocket money doing the lawns up at Feadan House."

"Good. I'll go out and show you the ins and outs of this make. Mind, it's never to be used without the guard. There's too much danger of flying stones."

Morag said wistfully, "I wonder why no one has ever invented motorized edge-clippers!"

Hazeldean chuckled. Really, when he laughed the man was almost human. "Your sister would no doubt remark that the reason was that, in the main, edge-trimming is a woman's job."

Lindsay shrugged, smiling. "I wouldn't, you know. I'm not a man-hater *in general*."

She saw by the look in Hazeldean's eyes that he had got her point.

He jerked his head at the children. "Off to brush your teeth, then meet me at the big green shed."

Lindsay felt as if the reins were slipping from her hands, yet there was nothing to cavil at, it was all done good humoredly. It was just that it would be so easy for this man to assume mastery in all things.

"Righto, Jock," said Callum. "C'mon, Morag."

Lindsay opened her lips to protest against this familiarity, then decided against it. He enjoyed baiting her.

But he had noticed. He reached up to the mantelpiece for his pipe. "Yes, better not. When in Rome do as the Romans do, and all that."

When she did not answer he grinned and added, "In fact, as we seem to be thrust together into the family circle, you'd better make it Jock too, Lindsay, or the kids, Neill included, will notice the enmity."

"The family circle is only a small one . . . the three Bairdmores . . . Neill, Morag, Callum. Not you or me. Though *I* am a half sister to two of them."

"You haven't got your facts right, Miss Macrae. I *am* family. Didn't you know I was Neill's cousin?"

Lindsay bit her lip, "I didn't know. But I get your emphasis. *I'm* the outsider, the only one with no connection with the estate."

"Well, you said it, not me. Touchy as they come, aren't you?"

He put his pipe down, came across, stood so close to her that he towered above her and she had to look up.

"Lindsay, the thing all newcomers learn when they come to New Zealand — or to any country — is adaptability. It's been an awkward situation, still is a bit, in the matter of you and me standing as guardians of the children and neither of us married. There are adjustments to be made. Yes, on both sides. Better make it Jock."

Lindsay realized in a flash what lay behind this. He was trying to disarm her. It hadn't mattered to him yesterday when he had thought — evidently — that he might be able to drive them away. Today he realized they had a right to be here and he thought it safer to be outwardly friendly, so that she would not suspect there had been any fiddling with the farm accounts. She had his measure all right.

121

"I just can't think of you as Jock of Hazeldean," she said, and knew it to be childish.

He strode to the door, leaving an impatient sigh in his wake. To her surprise he heeled round as he reached it and his eyes were dancing with laughter. "Then I give you leave to make it Euan," he said.

Yes, the man would bear watching.

4

NEILL was home by half-past four. He came straight into the kitchen, saw the oatcakes cooling on a rack, gave her a bear hug and said, "Gosh, this is good! Not much fun at exam time coming home to store-bought biscuits and having to make tea. And the lawns are done, edges and all. Who did 'em?"

He was spreading the oatcakes with creamy yellow farm butter.

"Say, this butter's homemade! Who did that?"

"I did. There was only commercial butter in the fridge and a lot of sour cream in the dairy. I just did a wee bittie, with the eggbeater."

"Good show! I love it, but we hardly ever bother. There's not much point — with the subsidy the government gives it's cheaper to buy. But I sure do love it for scones and pikelets and things. Gosh, I could eat a million of these. What's for dinner?"

"Stuffed leg of mutton — Mick boned it for me — peas, mint sauce. I dug some new potatoes, but they're woefully small. I hope Mr. Hazeldean doesn't mind."

"What, Euan? He'd better not. And dessert?"

"Apple pie."

"Gee willikins, how beaut! We've been living on canned fruit. I love pie. Do you think Mick could have dinner here too. Is the pie big enough?"

"Of course, I took it for granted he'd eat here while his wife's away."

"Gosh, it was a stroke of luck you turning up like this. We nearly died, thinking you'd arrive expecting house staff and whatnot, and all you'd have meant would have been another man to cook for. I bet Euan was tickled pink when you turned up. And I got myself another sister! Hey, what's the matter, Lindsay? I've made you cry!"

Lindsay put up an impatient hand to brush the tears away. "It's just stupid, Neill. It's just that I — I was so terrified you'd resent us, me in particular."

"You prize chump! It's no fun being

an only one. I'm thrilled. I only wish dad had brought you out years ago. Secretive cuss, wasn't he?"

Lindsay blew her nose, took off her apron and said, "Well, I'll have a wee walk around the garden, Neill. I'm itching to look around, but I've been so busy. It will cool me off. Tell me, how did the exam go?"

"Oh, not too bad. A lot of mapdrawing, and that's what I love. But the English paper the other day was a real stinker. Though I might just scrape through. It's maths tomorrow, so I won't have much studying to do tonight. I'll go hunt down the kids. I'm going to take them up Chophead Gully to see if we can see any wood pigeons. They're bigger than ordinary pigeons, you know."

"You don't mean you're going shooting?"

"No. Besides, they protected birds. Nobody shoots the *kereru*. They're beautiful . . . lovely coppery and green sort of iridescent plumage with white breasts, and frightfully tame. I've an idea that for special occasions the Maoris are allowed to shoot them. I'm not really sure. But this is just bird-watching. Euan's keen on that."

"All right. Dinner will be at six. Your cousin said that's the usual time."

"Okay."

* * *

As they rose from the table Euan Hazeldean said, "Well, Mick, you go along to see Wynne. Tell her I'll come to see her next week. Now, Morag and Callum, we're going to do the dishes. Neill, you take Lindsay over the hills and faraway. You don't need to study tonight, do you? She's been stewing in the kitchen all day, and it's not her rightful sphere."

Mick turned at the door. "Bit off beam, aren't you, Jock? After a dinner like that!"

"It wasn't a reflection on her cooking, Mick. I mean that she's a farmhand."

"What? Fair go? No kidding? Well, aren't we in luck! Help inside and out. You certainly got a winner in your new cousin, didn't you?"

He didn't disclaim this exaggerated

126

relationship. Yes, he must have decided it would pay to be on friendly terms. On guard, Lindsay!

She accepted his offer to help with the dishes. She was longing to get out to view this new land. And she was certainly sick of cooking.

As they left the room Hazeldean called out, "Put her up on Rosabelle, Neill."

Lindsay turned. "I can just take one of the ponies, thank you."

"You'd find them pretty slow. Don't be silly, take Rosabelle."

"Very well." Suddenly she grinned. "You certainly do go for Walter Scott, don't you?"

"Aye. He was one of my mother's favorites. We were brought up on him. She came from the Scott country."

Nostalgia, swift and unexpected, swept Lindsay for the valley of the Tweed, sunlit, leafy, dear and familiar . . .

Rosabelle was a handsome chestnut, with a white star on her forehead and one white foreleg. It was good to feel the movement of a horse under one again. Lindsay decided it was much to be preferred as a means of transport, to traveling in the plane over unfathomed depths of dark and strange oceans and cloud-wreathed, jagged mountain peaks.

Beyond the homestead garden and home paddocks, the country widened out with sweet green pastures dotted with white sheep and lambs, sweeping up the lower slopes of the tawny, crouching hills. The little lochan was stained pink with the sunset, they picked their way through the rocks and blossoming thyme.

"Euan said we were to open all the gates — I don't usually bother," Neill told her.

"You mean you just put the horses at the fences? So do I. I learned to ride very shortly after learning to walk. He wouldn't know that. We won't bother with the gates, Neill."

He shook his head. "Sorry, sis. Better to do what he says. It saves trouble in the long run. But we'll tell him next time."

Lindsay knew she must not encourage Neill to disobey his cousin and guardian. The 'Sis' warmed her heart.

"Which is Chophead Gully?" she asked. "And how did it come by such a horrible name? Or is it not as bad as it sounds? I mean it could be just a nickname for a tree or shrub or something?"

"No, it had a bad history, all right. I don't know how much you know of the history of this place a hundred years ago. There was no gold mining done on our flat land, but plenty back in the gullies. They were lawless days, of course, they jumped each other's claims, fought madly about it, were jealous of any good strike, and it was quite a common sight to see bodies going down river — not all victims of flooding. There was a fearful shindy up the gully one night. Some men were murdered and their decapitated bodies were found in the Clutha."

Lindsay shivered. It was hard to imagine in this smiling fertile land.

Neill went on, "Have a look over the old Accommodation House on the property sometime, Lindsay. The family made a bundle out of that, in their time. You'd find it interesting. Euan's always saying we ought to furbish up the stuff there and send some into the Museum. In one room there's all sorts of bits and pieces — old claim-pegs, horn whisky glasses, gold scales, miners' boots, cradles, all the mining gear. And one room with bars. The gold coaches had to come through under escort, you know, and there was often a prisoner. This was the only stone building for miles, so they used one room as a lockup."

They brought their mounts to a stop after a good gallop, and Lindsay gazed around. She pointed across the ribbon of the tar-sealed main highway, to where she could see a tiny gleam of orange-painted roof. "Would they be our nearest neighbors?" she inquired.

"Not really. Just the only ones in sight. The Fords are nearer. Their place, Westering, joins ours. See that shoulder of far hill? That's the natural boundary. We've got a bridge over the creek there. There's a lot of coming and going between the two places. There are stepping-stones farther down, but mostly we just walk the horses through. But Madeleine Ford is away just now. She just about lives here when she's home. The place you can see is Linmuirs'."

Lindsay turned the other way. "And what's that bigger creek . . . the one that comes down that hill and then broadens out? I can see a gleam of silver."

"That's the Hazel Burn."

"Hazel Burn? What a coincidence . . . your manager's name being Hazeldean."

"Oh, it's no coincidence. It was named after his family in pioneer times. There has always been a Hazeldean here with the exception of the years after Euan's father died and before he came back.

Lindsay sat very still on her mount, one hand arrested in its caressing of the mare's neck.

"Always a Hazeldean here? You mean they once *owned* Rhoslochan?"

"Yes, but times weren't good when Euan's father died, and he was only ten. My dad had just got married and was looking for a place. My mother was Euan's mother's youngest sister. So dad bought it. Mrs. Hazeldean — Aunt Helen — moved to Dunedin, went back to teaching, and came back here when my mother died. Euan used to come for holidays. He went to Lincoln College — an agricultural one — and then went shepherding in the high country. Then he took on being manager. The chap

131

dad had when he had his trip home — and met your mother — wasn't much good. And dad was always away a lot, in Dunedin. Euan was born at Rhoslochan, born in the tower room. Have you seen it?"

Lindsay nodded dumbly. Hazeldeans had been here for generations. But for the fact that his father had died young, Euan Hazeldean would have inherited Rhoslochan. No doubt when he went shepherding in the high country — the place to save money for your own farm, he had said — he had dreamed of buying Rhoslochan back. And she supposed either Lex wouldn't sell, or it had been valued at a colossal price.

Had he — this was the vital question — expected to have been left a share in it, in return for which he would look after Neill, perhaps even expected a fifty-fifty basis? Instead of which Callum and Morag had turned up, co-inheritors with Neill. No wonder he had resented their coming.

Perhaps Lex Bairdmore had promised him a share. Perhaps it had been left that way in a former will, rendered null and void by this last one. He had hoped that by stopping them in Scotland he might have been able to swing things to his own advantage more easily? Naturally enough it might have left a core of bitterness. But you had to accept these things, just as she had had to accept the setback of no legacy for herself, a legacy she would have neither wanted nor needed had she not had the children to care for, had she not been cut off from earning.

Nonetheless, she must not let sympathy for Euan Hazeldean's disappointment blind her to the fact that there seemed to be some funny business going on. Of course he might delude himself by arguing that a share was morally his, anyway. But she must not allow the children, in any way, to be cheated out of their inheritance.

Lindsay came soberly home.

* * *

On Saturday Neill was full of fun, relaxed and relieved that exams were over.

Euan Hazeldean looked after him reflectively. "I'm grateful the twins turned up, after all. They've taken Neill's mind off his father's death. It isn't good for young ones to brood. They have to learn that life rushes on, notwithstanding."

After all. That was admission that he hadn't wanted them. Yet he treated them well. Of course it was a case of accepting the inevitable.

She heard a strange step coming across the concrete yard and turned.

Hazeldean said, "Oh, hello, Mrs. Ford. Come to look the newcomers over, have you? This is Lindsay Macrae, half sister to Morag and Callum, my new cousins."

Mrs. Ford chuckled. "No, don't. It sounds like one of those horribly complicated relationships I can never make head nor tail of!"

"Oh, it's quite simple. Lindsay and I are not related in any way whatever."

Very blunt. He didn't want any suggestion of relationship.

Mrs. Ford shook her head at him. "You daft creature, Jock Hazeldean! Why in the world don't you spread it abroad she *is* a sort of cousin, then you wouldn't be needing to sleep in the *whare.* As it is, you probably do look on each other as cousins." She grinned. "But I won't mention that to Madeleine. It would give me still another angle to prod her with. Do that girl good to have me say she might be about to experience a stab of jealousy, what?"

Euan Hazeldlean grinned back. "If you're not careful, Fordsy, you'll be so much of an archconspirator, you'll get in a tangle you can't undo."

"Not me. I know Madeleine." She paused. "We aren't being mannerly, Lindsay. I'm going to call you Lindsay straight off — you're just about my Madeleine's age. She's away, but she'll be across next week to see you. I would have been here before, but I've been in Dunedin for a few days. I must tell you all about our scheme for marrying Madeleine off. Remind me. How are you managing, dear? Finding it much different from England? Well, Scotland, Jock, what's the difference?

"Have the children started school?" she went on. "They'll soon settle in, it's wonderful how children do. Just strange for a day or two, then squabbling happily with all the rest. How wonderful you turned up the day Wynne went to Clyde for her baby. She got a wee girl at last, how lovely. You can't have any more than two kinds. I had only one of each, but what does that matter when there are no more varieties? Like that man who let us have his seaside cottage up at Kaiteriteri, near Nelson, in exchange for ours at Queenstown . . . he wrote a preliminary letter in which he said, 'Has it enough bedrooms for all sexes?' I wrote back and said, 'Well, only enough for two, really, but I think you'll get by.'"

She paused. "Where was I? Well, it doesn't matter. I'll remember in a moment. How've you got on with the stove, or do you just use the electric? Very handy to know how to manage an old coal stove, because in this place, you never know. Power poles get blown down all over the place with high winds, or cut off by snow, or something and then where are you?

"If ever I think anything's dopey, it's getting rid of old coal stoves and depending completely on electricity. I always like two strings to my bow.

Now what are you laughing at, Jock Hazeldean?"

"At you, darling. I think this time you've got one string too many. I'm sure Madeleine sees through it and it isn't accomplishing a thing. Better just let me handle it."

"Never in your life! Diplomacy's not in a man's line at all. Men are about as subtle as steamrollers, don't you think so, Lindsay? It takes a woman. Men are so transparent."

This time Lindsay managed to get a word in. "I wouldn't agree with you there, I'm afraid."

She caught the manager's eye . . . and meant to. Better he should know she held a watching brief for the children and that her suspicions were already aroused. It might stop him getting in too deep.

"Anyway," said Mrs. Ford, "we can do without you now, Jock, we'll get to know each other much better without you interrupting all the time."

He gave a great shout of laughter and departed.

Lindsay didn't so much as take Mrs.

Ford into the house as was propeled inside by her.

Mrs. Ford looked around appreciatively. "My word, this is something like. Helen would be really pleased. I had a letter from her last week. She's wearying for her own place, of course, but she'd never let Elizabeth down. Imagine triplets. That's really overdoing it, but then Elizabeth's like that. Still, it's sort of balanced the family a bit. She had two girls first, now three boys. But can you imagine the routine?

"They all sit down with a baby each, Helen, Elizabeth, David. One is a much quicker feeder than the others and they all try to grab that one. There's such a difference in the time, they've made out a roster and take the fast feeder in turns. Good job the others are past the toddling stage — Linda is six and Christina four. Still, now you're here she won't worry about Jock and Neill and the homestead."

She looked round.

"I see you've been at the garden. I noticed you'd weeded the bed of ranunculas and anemones. Lovely, aren't they? Such a patch of color. But Helen put her sweet peas in far too early — I told her that — they'll be over long before her gypsophila is out, and they do look lovely together, don't you think? And much easier to arrange. They flop without. Somethings do go together — bacon and eggs, strawberries and cream, steak and kidney.

"Just like Helen and me. We were bosom friends. When Madeleine was born I said, looking at Euan, wouldn't it be lovely if they married and we became related? So ideal. And her so fair . . . well, red, really. With adjoining estates and all. I got even more keen on the idea later when I realized Max, my boy, wasn't keen on farming. He's got ticks in his blood."

"Ticks in his blood! My goodness, are your sheep very infested with ticks?"

Mrs. Ford stared, then went into gales of laughter. "Oh, you darling pet! No, I mean his grandfather — my father — was a watchmaker and jeweler, and that's all Max ever thought of. He's got a business of his own in Dunedin. We do have some trouble with ticks, of course, but nothing like in Australia. We use mostly spray dips these days, they're much more effective, and not nearly so distressing for the sheep as the old bath style. Cuts down on the cursing too."

"Cursing?"

"Oh, they still let it rip it a bit, especially when they're getting lambs through the race, but somehow it's not the pandemonium the old dipping used to be, and the fewer incidents, the less the men swear. Most of the old dips are filled in, it's much safer where children are concerned. Do you ride?" she went on. "Madeleine takes prizes in the shows. She's at her best on a horse. That was why she didn't want to fall in love with Duncan Besterman. He's an artist. Roves all around New Zealand and the islands of the Pacific. Always will. He'll never settle anywhere. I mean you can't ride a horse on a coral atoll, can you?"

"No, I suppose not." Lindsay was feeling dazed by now, not sure of anything.

"I can see what would happen. She'd always be looking back here in her mind, being homesick, knowing she could have married right on the spot. She needs pushing. That's why I keep telling her how suitable it would be if she married Jock, how safe, how secure. Never do to marry a nomad, I tell her. Good technique, eh? No uprooting at all, I keep telling her. Have the hills and paddocks and life you love. Well, time will tell. Tell me, did you make that bread sitting up in the rack? Well, I never!"

"Oh, Neill forgot to get some extra in Alexandra and I thought we might be short," Lindsay explained. "There was some yeast in a bottle — not proper stuff, medicinal stuff that Lex had taken, Mr. Hazeldean said. But it had a recipe for bread on the outside. You mixed it with bran and sugar. I think it's going to be rather nice. It's still a little warm."

"I tell you what, love, let's just have that for afternoon tea. I adore homemade bread, but I never get time. I've done it once or twice in snowstorms. Farm life is easy these days, everything just left in the mailbox."

Oddly enough Mrs. Ford wasn't exhausting, only entertaining. She was so uncritical you felt she liked you, and it was certainly no strain to keep the conversation going. She was much easier to get on with than that awful breed of people who were so reserved you had to keep thinking, *What on earth can we talk about next?* . . . something that always had a drying-up effect and left one far more exhausted.

But one pitied Madeleine, being hounded toward marriage. It sounded as if Euan Hazeldean favored it. As well he might — with a farm at stake. Perhaps he believed in two strings, too! If you don't inherit a farm, marry one!

The children went to Crannog School, found their first week a little trying and the lessons rather different, but as the school year finished here the week before Christmas for the summer holidays, which lasted till the first week in February, it wasn't a bad time to start. They would be one of the herd by the time they started the first term of the New Year.

Then tension between herself and Hazeldean had eased a little. She felt she was earning her keep looking after the house. She'd got most of the mending

done, had cleared two or three flowerbeds
of weeds, and staked the delphiniums and
perennial phlox against the might of the
winds that swept down through the river
gorges at times, through Cromwell and
Alexandra to Crannog.

She had had several letters from home.
She enjoyed Mrs. Rollinson's most of all
and smiled over one paragraph.

Mrs. Lockhart refuses to admit Robin's
engagement is broken. She insists it's a
tiff that occurred, most unfortunately,
as you were about to go overseas. You
know what a one she is about money.
The thought that she quarrelled with
you just when you were about to have a
legacy rankles. Watch her, don't let her
soften you toward Robin. He's tarred
with the same brush. Though I don't
know what harm she can do you so
far away.

So Lindsay wasn't surprised to have a
letter from Robin. He was cautious, not
asking her straight out to reconsider her
decision, merely hoping she was more
like herself and saying that though once

it seemed the end of the earth, now New Zealand was but a few days' journey. And he'd like to hear from her. Lindsay thrust his letter into the heart of the fire in the stove. She was carving out a new life for herself in a young, vigorous country, and she never wanted to see Robin or his mama again.

She and Mick had a grand clean-up of the cottage ready for Wynne's homecoming. The builders had almost finished building on the two rooms. The cousin who had the other three children was going to keep them, she said, till Wynne had got her sea legs with the new baby.

Lindsay was even grateful for the power failure when some lines were blown down when the men were all at Cromwell one day. They had offered to take her, but she was busy making rhubarb jam and wouldn't go. She had been using the electric stove, but switched to the coal one when the power went off. Then, she realized that if it was off for long they'd have to milk the cows by hand, and they were going to be late as it was.

So she got the cows in early. This

would show them it was handy to have a farm girl around the place. Then when Euan's mother came back, they might still find her useful.

She was just finishing separating as they came in over the cattle stops. They'd heard about the power failure in town, so were most relieved as they came up to the shed, wondering why the cows weren't waiting about to be milked.

Mick said, "Weren't we in luck, Boss, that we got a milkmaid as well as a housekeeper! Lindsay, you're an answer to prayer."

"Thank you, Mick," she smiled. "It's nicer than being called a cuckoo in the nest."

Mick looked puzzled as he moved off.

Hazeldean caught up with her at the house door. "Did you *have* to say that?" he asked savagely, and walked away.

She swung round, looked after him. He'd looked genuinely hurt.

She ran after him, caught his arm.

He turned round, the dark face looking down into hers.

"I'm sorry, Euan. I know things have

been more harmonious — even if they are still a little awkward — I mean my presence keeps you out of your room. But never mind. I'll find a solution to that soon, I think."

He looked at her sharply. "Have you been looking at places to rent in Alexandra when you've been in with Neill? Have you? Because you — "

"No — it was just that I — oh, well, I had an idea. I don't want to say anything yet. It wants thinking out."

He said slowly, "You have pulled your weight. I've got to admit that. We've not had it so good since Mother went away to Elizabeth's. And it's been a godsend, as Mick said, with Wynne away. Mick had to tell me, earlier, that Wynne wouldn't be able to do anything up at the house once she got the baby."

Lindsay said, "I don't know how she managed it as it was."

"No. She's a great worker. And of course she liked the extra money. Like all the married couples, they dream of a place of their own some day. No man worth his salt wants to be a hired man forever."

146

She looked up at him quickly, looked away. Then, not looking at him, she said carelessly, "Ever thought of having a place of your own, Mr. Hazeldean?"

"Yes, often." He came around face to face with her. "Lindsay?"

His nearness and height always overpowered her. She looked away again to the distant hills. He made an impatient noise, forced her chin up. His thumb was in its faint cleft.

Her hair, neither brown nor fair, caught back in its simple ponytail, waved softly at her temples. Her gray eyes regarded him steadily.

"Yes?"

The grooves in the dark cheeks were very distinct, running all the way to his chin. They made him look stern. His eyes were more green than hazel today.

"I like to have people look at me when I speak. What's the matter?"

She sounded a little breathless. Then she grinned. "You loom so! It's like standing under a tower. It makes me feel browbeaten."

He put back his head and laughed. "Browbeaten — you! You're more than capable of holding your own. You remind me of our bantam cock for all the world. Ever noticed that he's more than a match for our big white leghorn?"

She couldn't help it, she laughed. It was true. Lindsay had an air of fragility almost, with her perfectly oval face and blue-veined temples, but her mother had always said,'Oh, Lindsay, you're like one of my own folk, one of the fighting Lindsays.'

"That's better," said Hazeldean. "I thought you had a sense of humor somewhere. Mislaid it a bit since coming to New Zealand, had you?"

She sparked a little. "That's not a nice remark . . . nobody likes to have their sense of humor questioned. Would you have expected me to be gay and lighthearted? It's taken me some time to recover from being called a cuckoo in the nest and a vul — "

His hand came over her mouth, not gently. "Lindsay Macrae, you are not to use either of those terms again! I've changed my mind about you quite considerably. You'd not blame me, surely, for thinking you'd come out here

148

after the pickings, after all these years? But even in this short time I've realized that whatever happened all those years ago that ought not to have happened, you aren't to blame, and you are trying to pull your weight. Naturally it must have seemed a solution to you . . . a home and income for the children — "

He looked at his watch.

"But this is not the time and place for talking things over. I expect the milking made you late for your dinner duties. I'll come and peel the potatoes for you, as you've done my job . . . and done it well."

Lindsay was amazed at the glow of pleasure that spread through her. She said, "Oh, I had a good start. There was a casserole in the oven, so I switched it to the range, and there was some rhubarb over from the jam, so I made a pie, and the twins did the potatoes. It's ready to serve. But we got off the subject. I'm sure you were going to ask me something when you swung around, Mr. Hazeldean. What was it?"

He burst out laughing. "You've certainly reminded me. I was going to say that

149

when you ran after me to apologize you called me Euan very naturally. Why not always? Both Mick and Neill have remarked that you still use my surname.

Lindsay turned pink. "I hadn't noticed I used it."

"That shows how natural it was. Keep it up. I don't want any talk, don't want anyone thinking relations are at all strained in the household. They think it odd enough as it is, Lex having children in Scotland that no one knew anything about."

They heard the clippety-clop of hooves, turned, saw a rider take a fence with perfect grace and make toward them. It didn't need Euan Hazeldean's exclamation of "Madeleine!" to tell Lindsay who it was.

Who else could it be? She had come from the direction of the boundary creek. They made a lovely picture, the mare and the girl. She came to a stop near them, swung down. She was about the same height as Lindsay, but beside her Lindsay felt drab, mouse colored, insignificant. The other girl's coloring was so glorious — hair like a newly minted penny, eyebrows naturally dark above eyes that were almost violet, delicately shadowed in a way that owed nothing to art. Her mouth was a cupid's bow, her nose patrician. She had superb confidence.

"Hello, Jock. I've been home an hour. Couldn't wait to see you. How about coming over for the evening tonight? Sorry, how impolite of me. You must be Lindsay. My mama is raving about you. She said you were a wonderful conversationalist, which probably means you wisely let her have her head and she gave you a real ear bashing! What a blessing you arrived just as Wynne went off to the hospital. Sorry I was away, Jocko, I thought she was having it later."

"So did we all. No, I'm sorry I can't come over tonight. I'll make it tomorrow night. Lindsay and I are going to round up the sheep tonight. Lindsay is a trained farmhand, Madeleine. Isn't it luck? And I've been out all afternoon, so has Mick, and with a power failure poor Lindsay's been stewing over a hot stove making jam, and finished up by milking the cows by hand to save us when we got back. You knew the power was off?"

"Yes, mother's got the stove stoked up, too. Well, in that case I'll be off. You'll want your dinner early if you've to go round the sheep yet. Need any help?"

"No, thanks." Lindsay thought his tone was deliberately offhand. "The two of us will manage nicely, thanks. No chore on a night like this, and — " he smiled meaningly in Lindsay's direction " — with some company."

Madeleine sprang into the saddle, smiled charmingly and with no hint of offence, said, "I'll come back and have a yarn with you, Lindsay, when business isn't so pressing." She wheeled the big mare around, pressed her sides with her heels, rode off.

Lindsay looked at Euan Hazeldine. "I think I'm being used, aren't I? Between you and Mrs. Ford? I'm not at all sure I'm going to play."

"Oh, help," said Hazeldean unrepentantly, "don't let's start another argument. If you can withstand Fordsy's pressure, it's more than I can. Fact is I'm starving. And I do want you to go round up the sheep with me. Mick is going to get on with the lining of that room. If it's finished, there won't be hammering to wake the baby when Wynne gets home. I'll help him paper it — papering is noiseless, praise be."

Despite herself Lindsay found herself looking forward to the ride. She liked housework, but the pity was there was always too much of it for the hours of the day. This was a big house and it was so beautifully designed that it called out all the energy you possessed to keep it as it should be kept.

A shame then that the ride was spoiled for her near the end.

The night was warm and below them, the lochan brooded, not pink now, but rippled pewter. They had come up a slight rise and paused. Their horses had drawn close together till suddenly Lindsay became aware that Euan Hazeldean's knee was warm against her own, fitted neatly into its curve. She thought he seemed completely unaware of it. The horses had done it, she was sure, fidgeting around, and she was also swiftly vexed to find she liked the feel of it — more than vexed, horrified. She didn't want to feel those things any more, reminding her too vividly of the days when she thought Robin Lockhart the acme of all her dreams. She held herself rigid, not wanting to pull away abruptly, or to let him know she was aware of his nearness.

He suddenly looked down on her, and said, "You've got a sprinking of freckles too, like Morag. I hadn't noticed them, consciously, till this moment."

Why should a lightly made remark like that make her immediately self-conscious and gauche like an immature schoolgirl?

She ought to have laughed and said, 'A case for bleaching, I think.'

Instead, she moved abruptly, said, her eyes on the sheep clustering together on another rise, "How have wool prices been?"

"Extremely good. Better than for some time. In fact, since the peak year of 1950. This last sale was a surprise to everyone. I've ordered myself a new car on the strength of it."

Lindsay couldn't speak for a moment. He must have said it carelessly, off guard.

She moistened her lips. "*You've* ordered another car. You mean for the estate?"

He didn't reply immediately. Then he said, "Of course. What else could I mean?"

She said slowly, "I thought it might be a New Zealand custom to allow a manager to run a few sheep of his own on the place. But it would take more than a *few* fleeces to buy a new car, wouldn't it?"

"Yes . . . unless a man had a car in extremely good condition to trade in."

She said carefully, "I haven't noticed a car other than the Holden station wagon and the farm truck."

"You're dead right. There isn't one . . . apart from those. When Lex was alive we had two. We were often out separately. But when I speak of getting a car I mean for the estate, of course. We change cars frequently, it saves depreciation and maintenance. As I'm completely in charge now, naturally I use the first person. When Lex was alive I used to say 'we.' Satisfied?"

"Not altogether. May I ask you a straight-out question, Mr. Hazeldean?"

"Yes. Fire ahead. I can't pretend to like your attitude, of course."

"Then do you, or do you not, graze some sheep of your own on this property?"

Out of the corner of her eye she saw the glint in his, noted his hands tighten on the reins that had been lying slackly on Rosabelle's neck.

"I do, Lindsay Macrae. Have you an objection?"

She ignored that. "Is it under agreement?"

"Jim MacWilson knows all about it."

"Did it go on — I mean did you do the same thing when Lex was alive? Graze sheep on Rhoslochan?"

"Of course. Surely you don't think I just started that when he died? If you have any doubts of me, my dear cousin-by-marriage umpteen times removed, I suggest you write to Jim, asking him. He'll be able to satisfy you completely."

"Oh, that's all right. I hadn't realized that there were so many — er — perquisites when one was manager, that's all."

"You're being deliberately offensive, Lindsay, and very tiresome. It's not much different from share-milking when all's said and done. You don't understand the give-and-take attitude between New Zealand farmers and their employees. Even Mick has his perquisites. It's usually the custom to give the married couple a couple of cows. They collect the creamery checks, get all their meat and milk free and wheat for their fowls, even if they run enough to sell eggs."

Lindsay dug her heels into Joris and was away. She didn't know what to make of it at all. It sounded fair enough, but was it just a glib explanation of what had been almost a giveaway? And what would be the use of applying to Jim MacWilson, an old friend of Hazeldean's?

He came after her, caught up with her, but not to continue the argument, evidently. Perhaps he thought it wiser to drop it.

The horses slowed to a walk. They made their way in silence, nearing home.

Suddenly Lindsay felt Joris gather himself together and put a spurt on. Taken unawares, she tried to rein in, failed and knew a moment of panic. They were so near the stables and the door was open and low. She would be brushed off.

She tried desperately to crouch, to really flatten herself on his neck, but the next moment she was caught by the shoulders in a grip that bruised.

"Kick your feet out!" Euan Hazeldean yelled urgently.

She kicked, felt herself dragged over the saddle, across to him, against Rosabelle's side, and in some miraculous way the next moment she was feet on the ground, leaning against Hazeldean, who had leapt down with her.

She staggered against him, gasping. Joris had bolted clean to the stable.

"Damn that animal!" swore Euan. "I clean forgot that nasty little trick of his. It's his one vice. But I was so mad with you seconds before that I forgot."

He looked down on her, his chin on her head. "You're trembling, and no wonder!"

Lindsay said dazedly, "How in the world did you manage it? Talk about the wild West!"

"Blest if I know. Just put in all I had, acting on instinct. It would have cracked your skull open. From now on you ride Rosabelle."

Gone was all her anger. How could you feel angry with a man who had just saved you from, at best, a nasty accident?

She said shakily, "No, I can't deprive you of Rosabelle, Euan. I feel badly enough that I turned you out of our room."

"That's better — back to Euan. Much more natural. Good out of evil, eh? You worry too much about me sleeping in the *whare*. It's worth it to have a good, if temporary housekeeper."

She swallowed. "You mean that when your mother comes back we'll have to go to Alexandra? Just continue drawing an income for the children from the estate?"

"No, we'll scrub that idea. It would be a pity to deprive Neill of a sister and brother now, and Callum is a born farmer, he'd fret away from the land. Besides, they're my wards, too, and they need a man's hand."

"I do *not* spoil them!" said Lindsay fiercely.

She felt him shake with laugher. His

hand came up, smoothed the top of her head. "I can feel your hackles rising," he said chidingly. "I didn't mean to even hint you did. I think you manage the twins beautifully. I still think they need a man in the family as well. Just as Neill needs a woman about. I meant that when Mother comes back you could give us a hand outside. Two women are no good in a kitchen, ever." He added regretfully, "But it will be months before Mother comes home."

So they came in fairly harmoniously. It even lasted till they were washing the supper dishes. Till Lindsay said suddenly, "But one thing, Euan, I will not be used by either you or Mrs. Ford in the matter of Madeleine!"

It was disconcerting to have him laugh. "I think you will, you know," he drawled. "Mrs. Ford usually gets her own way. Why not be sporting and go along with us? Madeleine needs a bit of prodding."

Lindsay said shortly, "I don't approve. I hate interfering people and I detest scheming ones. I like straightforward folk. Well, that's the last of the dishes. Good night."

He took his dismissal, went to the door, paused with his hand on its knob. "Would you like to slam it after me, Lindsay?"

As she got into bed she realized sleep wasn't like to come easily. His rescue of her from a dangerous situation had overlaid those moments of quite horrible suspicion that she had entertained there on the hill. Now they came riding back, black spectres. There was quite definitely something wrong.

5

FOR the next few days Lindsay
might have been observed to leave
the house quite often if anyone had
noticed. But no one did; not Hazeldean
himself, for he was very busy with the
sheep, so was Mick; not Wynne, absorbed
in her new daughter; and the children
were away at school most of the day.

One morning at teatime, when only
Euan was in, since Mick now took his with
his wife, Lindsay said when he'd eaten his
bannocks, "I've something to show you,
and ask you, Euan. Have you time?"

"Why yes, where?"

She was noticeably nervous. "Across at
the old Accommodation House."

"What have you found? I heard you
and Neill having a great old powwow
the other night about the museum stuff
over there. Have you unearthed some
treasure?"

"No. Euan, I'd rather explain over
there."

162

"Right. It's decidedly intriguing. What have you been up to?"

The phone rang just as they were leaving. Madeleine.

Lindsay positively snorted as she heard Euan say: "Sorry, no, I can't. Look, can't you work that darned projector yet? Well, I'll slip over and show you once again, you ninny. I've never known anyone so unmechanical. If only you could say giddap to it you'd be set, wouldn't you? No, honestly, it's not just my usual disinclination for a crowd of people, fact is, I'm taking Lindsay to the pictures in Queenstown tonight."

That was when Lindsay snorted.

He put the receiver down and grinned at her. "You ought to be careful. Madeleine might have heard that snort. It was only that I hadn't mentioned it to you."

"Mentioned it! Don't you mean asked?"

He didn't reply, but continued to grin.

She said exasperatedly: "I wouldn't care if it had any effect on Madeleine."

"That's what you think. Mrs. Ford and I think otherwise. Madeleine is getting very browned off with the constant mention of your name." He added, "And as you had the air, a few moments ago, of going to ask me a favor, you'd better not stand me up. Mick will come up to stay in the house with the children."

Lindsay dared not refuse. She shrugged, said, "Well, I'd like to see that picture, but I didn't dream you'd go that far. Isn't it right through the Kawarau Gorge?"

"Yes. That makes two gorges. Mick and Neill will see to the milking. We'll leave early. I'll give you dinner in Queenstown, and you'll be able to see the scenery in daylight that way."

"It's not really necessary," protested Lindsay. "I can see it some other trip in daylight."

"It's purely selfish, we like people to thrill over our scenery. Especially the lake. Lake Wakatipu. All right, let's go."

They went across the paddocks, following a track, to the old stone Accommodation House. They came up through a grove of trees on turf nibbled almost to lawn by sheep, came to a path of flat river stones roughly set in the grass.

What hands had laid them there? Lindsay wondered.

Just as they neared the back door Hazeldean stopped, said, "What the dickens . . . waltzing Matilda, you certainly look for work, don't you! Fancy gardening here! Nothing's been done to this since the nineties, I reckon."

He gazed at a small flower bed between the side path and back entry. It had been cleared of weeds and dug, and there, transplanted from the homestead garden, were cineraria seedlings and pansies, purple and brown, that had decided to go on blooming in spite of their uprooting.

Puzzled, he followed her in. He stopped in amazement in the huge kitchen. "What's this? A work of restoration? But for what?"

Her face was quite white, her gray eyes enormous. "Please Euan, I want to live here. With the children. Every night when you go out to the *whare* I feel more than ever a cu — "

"Don't say it." He advanced on her mock-threateningly. "Don't say it. If ever I'm sick of anything it's that phrase, cuckoo in the nest."

"Well, I feel bad about it. Not only that, but even with you out in the *whare* it could cause talk if it goes on too long. Besides," her face lit up, "I just love this place. It's so quaint. And in wonderful repair, considering. We won't use the front rooms, of course, the bar and parlor and so on, just these few at the back. And I'll still do the housework at the homestead and come up and cook your dinner every night. You could drop down here for your lunch. This won't take much doing, I'll have loads of time. But this would be *ours*. As the homestead can never be. I've enough in my bank account for some plain furniture. Please, Euan?"

It took a lot of talking, but finally she wrung consent from him.

"Well, try it as an experiment. If you find it too lonely you must come back. Or if you miss the luxury of Rhoslochan too much. Don't let pride stand in your way."

"It's not far from the homestead, we'll be able to see your lights from here. And on the main road there'll be cars passing all the time."

He was puzzled. "You'd honestly rather rough it here than stay on with us?"

"Well, we can't all live under the one roof. When winter comes you won't want to sleep outside as you're doing now. And we would be well settled in before your mother comes back. Then she wouldn't feel she was turning us out. That could be a difficult situation."

He cocked an eye at her. "You don't know my lady mother. She loves taking people under her wing, she ought to have had half a dozen children, not just two. She's a sort of universal grandmother. I'm most reluctant about the whole thing. Why not wait and I'll build you a small cottage near Mick's?"

"Oh, I couldn't involve the estate in that much expense. Please let me. We've been your reluctant guests for so long."

He looked at her. "You've not been happy? You haven't been able to forget your reception?"

"Only partly that. I don't like living on your bounty. I don't want you creating jobs for me. I want to be independent."

"You mean just live on the children's allowance from the estate?"

She said stiffly, "I don't intend to live on the children at all. I have a little till I can earn. In fact, I intend, if you approve, to keep poultry. Hens, ducks, geese. I'm good at it. I'll sell the eggs and the dressed birds — there's a terrific lot of traffic past here — I'll put a notice up. And I could send some to market, no doubt. Anyway, it would be sufficient for my own small expenses. And if I continue to clean the house and serve your meals, perhaps that would do in lieu of rent."

Euan Hazeldean swore. He looked at her and said, "I'm not going to apologize for that, Lindsay Macrae. You make me madder than any other woman has done in my whole life. What the heck do you think I am . . . a blasted landlord?"

She said, maddeningly calm, "No. But I presume the estate is run as a business, and — "

"Well, if you think you're going to pay rent, the deal's off. You can have this place and I'll pay you what I paid Wynne for looking after the homestead." He took a turn about the room.

The anger suddenly left his voice. "Lindsay, give up this idea. You've

168

spoken too soon, anyway. It's time we put what you do on a wage basis. I was being canny, wanted to see if the broom swept clean only when it was new. Housekeepers are well paid in New Zealand, they're so darned scarce. Keep on as we are doing and I'll pay you for the job. I was going to ask you just that the night we went to round up the sheep, but we got offside with each other."

"No. I refuse to keep you out of the house any longer. If you don't agree, Euan Hazeldean, I'll set about renting a house in Alexandra. That would mean I could take a job in town."

He tried another tack. "What about leaving it till Mother gets back? If you like then I could build on an annex to the house. Living room, bedroom, porch for Callum, kitchenette and bathroom. And if you want an income you could run your poultry up at the house."

Lindsay was adamant. "I want my own rooftree. I don't want to feel under an obligation. I want to feel secure. I love this already, it's so quaint."

From the look in his eye as he gave in, she thought he probably surmised she'd pine for the luxury of Rhoslochan in no more than a matter of weeks.

"But it will be on my conditions, Lindsay. You say you don't mind lamps. Well, I hate the things, because of fire. You can have it if you wait till I get the electricians to wire it. They're coming out tomorrow to finish the electrical fittings in Mick's new rooms. I'll ring them and tell them there's another job. And they can put in a phone extension . . . as much for our convenience as yours. And I'll put in an electric stove. No slaving over that ancient monster in one of our Central Otago summers. You've not experienced one yet. They sizzle. Anyway, the chimney will be solid with birds' nests."

"It was," said Lindsay meekly. "I cleared them out. They made lovely compost for the flowerbeds."

He gazed at her. "Is there anything you won't attempt?"

"Yes . . . things mechanical. I'm just as dumb as Madeleine in that respect. So thank you, Euan. But about the electric stove — that's an expensive item. I'll pay for it. I have — "

The fiery glint came into the hazel eyes under the overhanging brows. "You are not going to have it all your own way, Lindsay Macrae. You can have the Accommodation House to indulge your whim about it, but you can make no condition about what I — what the estate puts into it. Half the cost of the stove you've already earned in the hours you've put in at the house. And what's more there's plenty of furniture up at the house to start you off.

"Neill asked the other day if he and Callum could turn Lex's room into a billiard room. So we've got to get rid of that stuff. It's a good thing to have a games room where you have youths, it keeps them out of the townships where there isn't much doing and cards flourish and liquor flows freely. Lex was given that way, you know. I want to provide counter-attractions for Neill."

It was the first criticism he had ever voiced of his uncle-by-marriage.

He went on, "And there's a bit of stuff in one of the lofts. I've always thought it pretty good. A bit Victorian perhaps, even a little ornate but solid, and it would rather suit this place. I think mother said it was chucked out by a Hazeldean bride in the twenties. If you dislike it, okay, but it would save you money. Big chests of drawers, a mahogany table, leather-seated dining chairs. And if you want to run geese, for goodness' sake take ours. Since mother's been away they're just a blasted nuisance. Neill doesn't mind hens. And I'll pay you so much an hour for the time you spend on our house."

Lindsay had no course but to accept that.

The fact that they had both had to make concessions made for more harmony between them than had existed hitherto. Lindsay knew a lightening of the heart that she would have a measure of independence and that the manager would be able to take up his own comfortable quarters again.

She was tempted to try to settle in right away, but thought she'd better not rush things or neglect the homestead. So she made a cold dinner for the youngsters, putting a few festive touches to it, then went up to her room to get ready for the evening's outing as soon as they got in from school.

Apart from a parent-teacher meeting at Crannog School, this was her first social occasion.

Morag approved. "Wear your green frock, Lindsay, it makes your eyes look green, and your white jacket."

Lindsay laughed. "Hark to my little tomboy sister! Starting to take an interest in clothes, poppet?"

"Not for me, but at your age, Lin, it's pretty good. You aye dressed up for Robin."

Lindsay turned away, her fair skin flushing. It was the first time either child had mentioned Robin since they left Scotland.

Lindsay wasn't prepared for the feast of beauty that lay ahead of her. Here was no dreamy gentle beauty but grand and grim, looking as if it had been spewed up from the bowels of the earth in some cataclysmic upheaval. It represented more of a challenge than an invitation, as if it had said to the pioneers, 'Come, pit your wits against me, wrest a living if you can,

but you may die in the attempt!'
Many had.

Alexandra was a tree-crowded oasis under the circle of bare relentless hills, the setting sun striking from rock and pillar blindly. Clyde dreamed under the lengthening shadows of great heights, then they took the Cromwell Gorge Road where the river savaged its way through harsh, pitiless hillsides with only here and there yellow tussock, incredibly dry; sometimes the heights plummeted down to the blue green water, sometimes they leveled out to plateaulike shelves where oases of living green spread themselves as testimony to the fact that men had taken up the challenge of the arid wastes and made the desert blossom as the rose.

Here were the fruit orchards: peach, apple, apricot, pear, all showing signs of set fruit. The orchardists' houses were mostly new, rather luxurious. Even in this heat there were still smoke pots between the trees, tribute to their fear of the heights that could still be snow-clad at times, even in November. The road threaded above the river with a low stone coping between it and the railway

174

that only went as far as Cromwell, Hazeldean said.

He drove slowly enough to point out the things of interest, the scars of the diggings, the heaps of shale, the rusty iron of old dredges protruding through the shingle. Here and there on the far side of the river would be an old poplar tree, with beside it the ruins of an old stone chimney. "Every gully bringing water down would be alive with miners. See . . . a cave, blocked up a little, to provide shelter from the elements. Rough, but better than canvas. Can you imagine tents in these screaming gales that whistle down through the gorges?"

She could occasionally glimpse the remnants of a loose stone wall. She shivered, "They must have had to crawl around some of those bluffs."

Just before crossing the bridge into Cromwell he paused to let her see the confluence of the two rivers. Cromwell was on a point of land between the two — the Junction, it had been called earlier.

"Ah!" said Hazeldean with great satisfaction. "Ideal conditions for seeing the way the two rivers run so fast that the waters don't mingle for some distance. You can always see it faintly, but tonight the Clutha pouring out from Lake Wanaka is slightly discolored, it must have been raining in the back country, and the Kawarau from Lake Wakatipu is still blue."

The two rivers churned together in foaming splendor, raced side by side, finally mingled. They crossed the narrow bridge, came up into the township with its church spires and pointed trees forming a symmetrical pattern against the brown hills beyond and the pearl and rose of the evening sky behind the far mountains.

At the racecourse where a tattered wind sock indicated an emergency landing field and the strength of the gales, they turned left; the right-hand fork led to Wanaka and the Haast Pass Road to the West Coast.

It seemed incredible that the Kawarau Gorge could be even more wild and untamed; here the river frothed and seethed in narrow chasms, forcing the water through in white fury. The Gentle Annie trickled down a hillside, but the

Roaring Meg jetted its waters through to join the river.

They came into Queenstown over the Shotover River with Coronet Peak, still white on its extreme tip, above them, its ski fields brown for the summer.

And there, cornflower blue, Lake Wakatipu lay, cradled in mountains, arms and inlets reaching out into far distances.

"You must fly over it some day so you can see its true shape. Some call it the dog-leg lake. I like the Maori legend that calls it the trough of the *tipua*. The Tipua was the monster who lay in the trough between the hills, sleeping in the northwest wind. Dry bracken and *manuka* were heaped on him and set alight, and while unconscious he drew up his knees. His head was Glenorchy, his knees Queenstown, his feet Kingston. It was said that all of him was consumed but his heart, which goes on beating, and that's supposed to cause the strange falling and rising of the lake, like breathing."

"How deep is it?" asked Lindsay.

"The maximum is about twelve hundred

feet. It's fairly cold — it remains between fifty-two and fifty-four degrees, summer and winter. I always think of it as Whaka-Tapua, the Hollow of the Giant."

For once they seemed at one, all past distrust forgotten in her delight at seeing such grandeur, in his at showing it to a newcomer.

Lindsay gazed up at the jagged peaks of the mountains that rose from the foot of the lake, silhouetted against the sky as sharply as if they had been cut with gigantic pinking shears. "What an extraordinary range of mountains!" she exclaimed.

His face creased into a smile as he drew to a stop for better viewing. "That's the perfect comment. They're called The Remarkables." He laughed. "One American called them The Unthinkables! I'm glad they've still got pockets of snow. This is the Frankton Arm — there's a small Presbyterian church there with a window looking right up the lake. The holiday cottages have spread to here. Now we'll go into Queenstown proper."

The road skirted the lake, it was

fringed with the most charming holiday houses with gardens as well tended as if people lived there all the year round. Above them motels and lodges climbed the hillsides. Larches and pines gave it a Canadian air, but the gardens blazed with English flowers, growing prolifically.

The township was different from any other New Zealand township Lindsay had seen so far. The streets were narrow the buildings close together, many of them washed with pastel colorings. "It's got almost a continental air," she said slowly.

Hazeldean nodded. "Yes, there was a certain influence in the early days. The gold drew people from all over the world. There were French and German folk here." Then he added what gave Lindsay her great idea. "From December to the end of March there will be thousands of buses and cars passing your door in the Accommodation House, Lindsay. Better change your mind, the traffic may keep you awake."

Thousands . . . and they would all want to eat!

★ ★ ★

The children were at first averse to leaving Rhoslochan, but they saw the manager must have his room back before winter and the novelty of the venture compensated them.

Lindsay, busy though she was, realized Madeleine was spending more time at Rhoslochan. Perhaps Mrs. Ford's scheme was working. Though she was sure had she been Madeleine, throwing her at the man's head would have worked the other way.

She said to Euan one day, "I came across to do your ironing, but Madeleine had done it. She was just leaving."

He narrowed his eyes. "You sound disgruntled. You don't mind passing that job up, do you? All this running between two houses must be tiring."

Her voice was scornful. "Disgruntled? Good heavens! You don't think Madeleine and I are exactly vying for your favors, do you?"

To her chagrin he burst out laughing. "Hardly. As you once remarked, Madeleine doesn't even seem to notice you're around. Poor Fordsy! She had these quaint ideas."

Lindsay said, her tone edged, "Anyone as lovely as Madeleine needn't fear competition anyway. Mrs. Ford should import someone glamorous."

His mouth twitched. "What's this, Lindsay? An inferiority complex cropping up? It needn't. If only you'd go out and about more, you'd be married off in no time."

"I loathe the way you speak of marriage. It's so prosaic, so ordinary. No wonder Madeleine takes no notice. You're so cold-blooded."

"What?" He seized her wrist, his light tone gone. "Who says I'm cold-blooded?"

She stepped back. "*I* do. And you are. I don't just *think* you're cold-blood, I *know* you are. No ordinary girl would stand it, much less one like Madeleine. And let me tell you this. I didn't come here looking for a husband. I came to look after my little brother and sister. I'm not particularly interested in men."

"Not at the moment, perhaps, but you were, weren't you?"

"What do you mean?"

"This Robin Lockhart Morag talks about."

Lindsay went cold. "What does Morag say about Robin?"

"That you used to dress up for him. You were there when she said it."

Lindsay shrugged. "Oh, that!" She went to walk away. His hand fastened around her wrist, drew her back.

"Were you in love with Robin?" he demanded.

"Yes."

"Still?"

Suddenly Lindsay's lip quivered. She caught it between her teeth, controlled it, said in a level tone, "You ought not to have asked that, so I won't answer it."

He let her go.

She picked up a basket of mending to take over to their quarters.

He said behind her, lazily, drawling, "What technique do you advise for Madeleine?"

Her lip curled. "Is that the sort of thing a woman could teach a man?"

"I think so. You ought to know what women like, what they expect."

"Well, for one thing they don't expect to be treated so casually. You and Mrs. Ford between you are putting it on a comonsense basis. You grew up together, or practically, and the farms adjoin. Madeleine loves this life — sheep, horses, shows, the great outdoors. Therefore you seem to think that's all it needs. That she would fall in love with the life she likes. Yet, against her will she fell in love with this artist, did she not? Perhaps because *he* wasn't casual, wasn't cold-blooded. In fact, despite his way of life having no attraction for her whatsoever, she did fall for him. You won't accomplish a thing on a commonsense basis with Madeleine. I imagine she can predict to a certainty your every move. Women like the unpredictable, the surprising."

"Do they, by Jove?"

She was utterly unprepared for the lightning swiftness of his movement. The darning basket was wrested from her grip, dropped on the floor. She was seized, his fingers biting into her shoulders. She looked up into the dark face, the glinting eyes, gasped.

The next moment his mouth was on

hers. She was quite helpless, bent back in his arms. It wasn't a quickly-snatched kiss. It lasted a considerable time. When he did lift his lips from hers he did not free her. Just as well, for she would have fallen.

A wave of fury rose in her as she took in the fact that he was laughing.

Yet his eyes fairly blazed into hers. "Cold-blooded, am I? Predictable, am I? You idiot, issuing any man with a challenge like that! You certainly didn't expect that, did you, my Lady Oracle?"

She drew a hand across her lips; even the hand was shaking. Then she managed, "I certainly didn't. Otherwise you wouldn't have succeeded. I — I — " she found she couldn't go on.

She turned and walked to the door, blindly scattering wool and socks everywhere. She felt like running, but wouldn't let herself appear to fly from him.

As she reached the sanctuary of the Accommodation House she saw the mailman pull his van in and thrust mail into the box. She walked across to it. She would take her letters, if any, and leave his. He could collect his mail himself!

Her mail might take her mind of that — that ridiculous scene.

It did . . . temporarily.

She waited till she got into the kitchen before opening it. One long envelope, marked with the solicitor's name. But she had got the children's allowance only last week. Besides, this was fatter — she slit the envelope and drew out the contents.

Not a letter only but a document, too. Title deeds . . . deeding her the Accommodation House and the two acres of land surrounding it for her own exclusive use. She swayed a little, gazed at it unbelievingly, picked up the enclosed letter.

It was from James MacWilson and was very much to the point. Simply that as Lex Bairdmore had not lived long enough to make her the legacy she had been promised, the property mentioned in the deed of gift had been granted to her by the executors of the estate. They felt that morally she was entitled to some compensation for having brought the children right across the world.

Tears welled up. She brushed them

away impatiently. How ill-timed that scene had been. What could she do? How could she face Euan Hazeldean to thank him?

She dropped down on a kitchen chair, put her hands on the table and her head on her hands. She just couldn't go in search of him.

A meek voice from behind her said, "Please, I'd still like my socks darned. And don't tell me to take them to Madeleine! I just couldn't stand it."

She turned round, saw him filling the doorway, holding in front of him, like an olive branch, the darning basket. She caught his eye and knew she was going to laugh.

He advanced, dropped the basket on the table and said, "Thank the Lord you can now see the funny side of it."

She said, trying to control her laughter, "I didn't know how to meet you again. I never dreamed you'd come over to apologize!"

"I have *not* come to apologize! Heavens, what do you take me for? I may not know much about women — according to you — but only a cad would apologize for a kiss. Talk about an insult to a woman! But, Lindsay, don't ever take a risk like that again! Know what? . . . You haven't much idea how to treat men! Talk about provocative — Now, don't get mad again. We have to remember our children . . . all right, I mean our wards. It's just as bad for them to have us fighting as if we were their parents. And don't try to explain Madeleine to me. You don't have to. She's the most contrary, bewitching, exasperating girl I've ever known. And I'm not going to do a darned thing to help her make up her mind. She can make it up herself." His eye lit on the letter, shifted to her face, and their glances locked.

Then he said lightly, "So it's come, has it?"

She said ingenuously, "Yes, it made me cry. I didn't know how ever I could find courage to come and thank you. After — after that."

They both laughed again, and he said quite seriously, "Then it's just as well I came to you."

"I — I don't know how to thank you. I realize the suggestion must have come from you. And — and there are other things. You supply our meat, our milk, the — "

He stopped her with an uplifted hand. "That's enough. You would have been having your share up at the homestead. This is working out all right — at the moment. You come up and cook our dinner and I have lunch down here, yet the living arrangements are much more conventional. And it means Neill is almost as much with his brother and sister as if they were still at the house. Well, Mick will wonder where I am. We're supposed to be clearing a water race." He got up. "Oh, and I rang one of the Queenstown hotels yesterday. They'll take all the geese and ducks you can fatten up for Christmas. Mick will kill and clean them for you if you can manage the plucking."

"I can clean them too. It was my job on my employer's farm back home."

"No, it's no job for a woman, that. Well, so long."

She stood at the window of the old kitchen watching him stride whistling through the trees and thought of his words about Madeleine. *Contrary . . . exasperating . . . bewitching.* They fitted Euan Hazeldean too! She heartily amended that in her thoughts. *Well, contrary and exasperating.*

Her thoughts wandered to other things he had said . . . and done. She pulled herself up with a jerk. Heavens, what had come over her? Just because they had shared a laugh . . . and a kiss . . . it didn't mean he was altogether to be trusted. *Careful, Lindsay.*

Lindsay's heart said to Lindsay's mind, *But look at his generous gesture about the old Accommodation House. Deeding it to you.*

Her mind came back with, *But remember how easily women believe unscrupulous men, Lindsay Macrae! Even mother, so wise in all other things, fell for Lex. Even you yourself had been deceived in thinking Robin a man to lean upon, a man to ride the water with.*

Her first rush of delight on receiving the deeds was subsiding. Time now for sober reflection. That gift could be a sop, something to stop her prying too closely into the affairs of Rhoslochan. Lindsay felt an utter desolation at the thought. If only she had a brother, an uncle, a cousin to advise her!

It would hardly be wise, at this juncture, to engage a solicitor of her own to look into things. They had to live together on the estate, and for the children's sakes it must be in reasonable harmony.

Later that night in the long twilight of the South Island, when the children had gone to bed, she was wandering through the grove of trees, enjoying the cool of the evening and she looked up beyond the big house to the rise above Chophead Gully.

Two riders were silhouetted against the skyline. Euan and Madeleine. Then they moved downhill, close together. Lindsay thought they were handlocked.

Perhaps, after all, Jock of Hazeldean had benefited by her advice, was dropping his too casual air and taking advantage of the magic of the sunset, later perhaps, the moonrise.

Lindsay shivered suddenly. It must be growing cold. And where was the point in mooning about a garden by yourself?

Especially a garden like this, peopled by ghosts of lonely adventuring men, desperate, afraid, insecure.

Over the back door an old-fashioned briar rose glowed pinkly; beneath it, seeded from plants of a century ago, daisies glimmered whitely. Lindsay went in, shut the door quickly behind her.

A wind sprang up, moaned eerily through the dark pines outside, moved the old chains on the stone verandah. Ghostly noises . . . creakings. The house didn't seem to belong to her at all on nights like this. There was a stealthiness about it, something that belonged to its unsavory past. You were aware that back there, that barred room had known fear and misery; that in the bar had been rough miners, bawdy jokes, notorious women who had followed the pick and shovel. You could almost hear the clink and jingle of the harness of the gold coaches, the snortings and whinnyings of the horses.

What sort of a life was this for a young girl?

Lindsay shook herself mentally. It was only that Hazeldean had mentioned

Robin. That was it, and the kiss coming after it had disturbed her, reawakened longings she had put behind her.

There was no future in thinking of Robin, though, for the Robin Lindsay had loved hadn't existed at all.

Suddenly, with a flash of honesty, Lindsay admitted to herself that the thought of Robin hadn't disturbed her a whit.

The kiss had.

She brought her hand down on the kitchen table with a bang. That was perfectly ridiculous. Had she no pride? That kiss hadn't meant a thing to Euan Hazeldean. It was a matter of male pride, stung to the quick by her ill-chosen words.

So it wouldn't matter to her, either!

Lindsay went to bed.

6

IT was most fortunate that Neill had his license for driving and that he could take the Holden whenever Lindsay needed to go to Alexandra for shopping, also that he was anything but curious about her parcels. He was very keen to show the twins everything there was to be seen in and around Alex, so it was easy to get rid of them while she shopped.

Certainly the manager did come in to the Accommodation House once or twice, and caught her in a paint-daubed overall, but he merely thought she was continuing to do up the back rooms for them and didn't suspect that she had rushed through from the front when she heard him coming. She was careful at lunchtimes to keep the doors shut that led through. And she locked them when the children were expected home. Lindsay had no great faith in their ability to keep secrets.

By now she had the bar completely whitewashed and she had painted the insides of the window sashes, with their charming small panes, a pale blue. Thank goodness the outside didn't need painting. It would be sacrilege to attempt to whitewash those stones, they blended so well into the landscape.

Euan Hazeldean knew she had a passion for gardening, so he had said nothing beyond saying, "You certainly create work for yourself, don't you?" when he found her attacking the tiny front garden. It looked very trim now. The old garden at the house had yielded dozens of seedlings; the hollyhocks she had transplanted had suffered scarcely a check and were in bud; verbena and aubretia were flourishing; hardy marigolds filled up the bare patches; and cultivation around their roots, plus plant food, had perked up the ancient roses that writhed and clung everywhere.

The children had helped her clean out the incredibly filthy old hen houses at the back of the stables, and now they were whitewashed and tenanted. A tiny tributary of the Hazel Burn wandered through the old overgrown orchard, a paradise for the webfoots.

Lindsay put an order for furnishings and furniture through an Alexandra firm, and today she had bought a lot of china, but it would not arrive for a day or two. But she must tell Hazeldean her plan soon now.

That night when the children were in bed she heard his unmistakable step on the rock path. Despite herself her heart leaped. *Only because you're lonely for adult company,* she told herself.

His face was set when he came in. This time her heart leaped with fear. What could have happened? Had he found out what she was intending and was mad about it? She ought to have told him sooner, perhaps even asked his permission. Only she so valued her independence, and he might have insisted on providing some of the fittings.

He had something in his hand and slapped it down on the table.

"Perhaps you'd be good enough to explain this, Lindsay!"

Wonderingly, she gazed at it. A Post Office Savings Bank book.

"Whose is this?" she queried.

"I think you know. Neill's of course."

"How would I know?"

His eyes bored into hers. "You were in town with the three of them today, weren't you?"

"Yes, but — "

He snorted. "Open it," he said tersely.

She protested. "Does Neill know you've got this? I mean this is *his* business."

His chin jutted. "It's also *my* business. He's my ward. And the other two are my wards, too. I'll get to the bottom of this hanky-panky, I can tell you. Who put Neill up to it? Open up that book, I say!"

Bewildered, she opened it. Neill had drawn out exactly one hundred pounds. Today. No wonder Euan was angry. What could he have wanted it for? She saw that it left exactly fifty pounds. He'd earned this money with holiday jobs, she knew, because Neill had talked about going fruit picking and also because he'd said that during the holidays he worked at Rhoslochan and got paid.

"A hundred pounds! What on earth

would he want that amount for? What — "
a thought struck her with panicking force.
"Euan . . . he hasn't run away?"

"Of course not. He's in the billiard
room, having a few knocks." His eyes
were almost black and very brilliant. But
for the first time he was not so sure of
himself. The gray eyes looking up into his
were so limpidly clear. "Lindsay, don't
you know what he wanted it for?"

She shook her head. "I can't imagine."

He put his hand in his pocket and
drew out two more savings books, bright
orange ones. He laid them on the table,
opened them. There was the first entry in
each book date-stamped by today's date.
The amount in each case was the same.
Fifty pounds. One book bore Morag's
full name, one Callum's.

Her dismayed eyes came up to Euan's.
"I don't understand. How — what — I
mean — Euan, I wanted to do some
shopping on my own. So I told them to
scram and have milk shakes. That must
be when — but why? And — "

"Only one way to find out. It's all right,
Lindsay. Forgive my unjust suspicions.
I'll ring Neill from here."

He told Neill what he'd found. "I went into your room looking for my folding ruler and there were the three books lying on your bed. The newness of two of them attracted me, and I couldn't imagine what anyone would want three bankbooks for. I ought to have called out and asked you, I know, but I acted on impulse and opened them to see who they belonged to. And I thought it strange enough to ask Lindsay about. But she doesn't know a thing. What's it mean, Neill?"

He listened, said a sentence or two, nodded, then said, "That's fine, Neill. But why didn't you tell me — or Lindsay?"

A pause, then he said, "Now I get it. Of course! So simple. Right, see you later."

He hung up, turned to Lindsay. "I feel a heel, even questioning him," he said. "It was simply that he didn't see why he should have a hundred and fifty pounds and his sister and brother nothing. He'd like them to start off equal. He's very, very like his mother. So he just opened up an account each for the twins and divided his money into three. And — and when I asked him why he hadn't told us he quoted last Sunday's text at me. You know: 'Let not the left hand know what the right hand doeth.' Sometimes kids make you feel small, don't they?"

The tears just welled up in Lindsay's eyes. She tried to say something, but choked.

Euan Hazeldean smiled, put his arms around her. "I know . . . gets you by the throat, doesn't it?" He held her as a brother might, as the father she had never known. She fumbled for a handkerchief, and had one put into her hand.

His voice was rueful. "It's not even clean. I bent back a bit of barbed wire on a post coming over and scratched myself. I mopped up the blood with this."

Lindsay hastily scrubbed at her eyes with it, looked up. "When you were on your way here? Then it hasn't been attended to? Let me — "

He held her fast. "I'll fix it when I get back home, child. Don't fuss. I'm immunized against tetanus."

"That's all very well, but there are

plenty of other infections more likely to set in."

She slipped out of his grasp, went to the sink cupboards got a bowl of disinfectant, some medicated gauze, cotton wool.

He suffered her ministrations smilingly.

"It's in quite a nasty place, Euan Hazeldean. Had it been Neill who'd cut himself you'd have been fussing, too." She wound the bandaging firmly and said, "Euan, keep your head out of the way, I can't see it properly. What on earth are you doing?"

"Trying to decide what your perfume is. Not violets . . . not lavender . . . ?"

"Euan! Let me see the bandage. No, it's not nearly as simple. It's one of those stupid modern scents with equally modern names."

"Such as?"

"Oh, right daft names. But I liked this perfume despite its tag."

"Which was?"

She sighed. "You're so persistent! If you must know it was called Tantalization. Satisfied?"

He chuckled. "That perfume should suit you very well." He laughed again.

He had her by the elbows. "You're a mass of contradictions . . . you look so cool, so simple, so uncomplicated. You look as if you ought to smell of oatmeal soap and white lilac or clover. And you're the most tantalizing little devil I've ever known, do you hear?"

He drew her to him. She had picked up the bottle of mercurochrome to put the top on and it was perilously full.

She leaned away from him a little. "Euan, stop it this moment! I'll spill this, and I've got a good dress on."

"It's a very lovely dress. I've aye liked women in blue. So do nothing to jeopardize it."

He bent his head and laughed, his mouth two inches from hers, his eyes dancing. "Don't let's kiss in anger this time, Lindsay, it spoils the flavor. Didn't you know?"

She said, through gritted teeth, still carefully holding the red liquid aloft, "I'm not expecting to enjoy it in any case. Euan, will you stop this silly — "

She didn't manage to finish it. He began to kiss her. She dared not struggle. She was conscious of many feelings. To her horror she felt herself responding, yielding . . . Then they heard it . . . the opening of the door.

Euan released her so suddenly she had to clutch at the bench to steady herself. She set the mercurochrome down, spilling a little on the bench, knocked the roll of bandage off, and was glad to stoop to rescue it.

Then a voice, Madeleine's, said coolly, "Oh, sorry, folks. Am I intruding? Would you like me to call again?"

Lindsay made an effort to get in first. "I — I'm just bandaging Euan's finger.

Madeleine burst out laughing. "I'd have thought him too old for this kiss-it-better technique, you know!"

Lindsay turned peony red and could have enjoyed firing the whole lot, disinfectant, bowl and bandages, at both Madeleine and Euan.

Euan's answering laugh was as natural as Madeleine's "You always had a genius for turning up at the wrong time, Maddy. But now you are here you'd better stay. What did you want with me?"

"I wanted Lindsay, not you. Thought I'd like a pleasant, chatty evening with someone my own age for a change. My darling, devoted, matchmaking mama is getting on my nerves. She's been extolling your virtues, Jock, for the last hour or so, nonstop. I'm sick of it! Thank heaven I walked in on you just now. I can hie me back and tell her your interests are engaged elsewhere. What a godsend. I will *not* be shoved around like this!"

Lindsay decided Madeleine must be mad clean through, and it suited her. Her deep blue eyes bright, her cheeks carnation pink, her hair glinted pure russet.

Lindsay looked at Euan to find him, of all things, struggling with laughter.

"Look at Lindsay!" he gasped. "She doesn't know whether *my* feelings are hurt, whether jealousy is making you act like this, or what! In fact she doesn't know who she ought to solace first. It's all right, Lindsay. Madeleine and I understand each other. We always have. Let's all have a cup of coffee and leave the subject alone. We'll only make it worse if we discuss it. Then I'll see you home, Madeleine."

"You'll do nothing of the kind. I didn't

come over the paddocks. I came by car. I will not give mother the satisfaction of seeing you escort me. I won't even say you were here. Lindsay, I also came over to see if you'd take part in the institute play. We want someone with a faintly Scots accent. You would be able to exaggerate yours."

"I'm sorry, but I couldn't. I'm going to be busy."

Euan said, "The rehearsals will be in the afternoon, I imagine. It wouldn't mean leaving the children. Anyway they could sleep at home for any night rehearsals."

Here it comes, thought Lindsay. *Anyway, even if he's cross about it, he can't let go the same with Madeleine here.*

She cleared her throat. "I'm opening up a tearoom here next week. It's an ideal spot, and there's no other restaurant for miles. Already there's a lot of traffic past, and by mid-December it should be really good."

They both gaped.

"You're what?" demanded Euan Hazeldean. "In this great barn of a place? Why, you'd never get a permit. It would take a month of Sundays to get it fixed up."

"I've got the permit," said Lindsay quietly, "and I've managed all the preliminary decorating. Would you like to come and have a look? The furniture is arriving Thursday. The inspector came out the day you were at the Cromwell sale."

Euan's expression was grim. "Lead on," he said.

She went ahead, her knees like jelly.

She unlocked the door into the private parlor. She was pleased at their expressions of unbelief. It was charmingly done. Cool matting covered the floor, potted plants were everywhere, softening the bare outlines. They had cost her nothing: all ferns and ivy from the bush. Cinerarias glowed from bright plastic bowls, a pile of linen curtains lay on a table so highly polished Euan didn't recognize it for the derelict one out of the loft. There was a row of pewter mugs on the mantel, a view of Lake Wakatipu above it. On the walls were a few prints she must have picked up in Alex: one of an old dredge working the river, a large, very old map of the diggings, a colorful picture of Lake Hayes in autumn; one of the gorge near the Roaring Meg.

She took them through to the bar. The whitewashed stone walls gleamed, red geraniums sat on the pale blue sills, the shelves were fresh with paint and neatly lined with washable adhesive baize. One wall was covered with relics of the mining days, tacked up or hung from hooks. Anything that would polish had been rubbed till it was shining. Other antique bits stood on a long table. Neat little tickets were printed for each article, with its approximate date and use.

"All I lack is a genuine gold nugget," said Lindsay.

"Heavens!" said Euan. "The darned place is absolutely charming. But what are you going to serve?"

Lindsay went to a long board sitting against the wall, turned it. It said simply, Lindsay Macrae. Scottish teas, Oatcakes, Bannocks, Girdle-scones, Pancakes. Jam and cream. Reasonable charges. There was a painted sprig of heather at one end of the sign and a bow of the red

Macrae tartan at the other.

"Who painted it for you?" Euan demanded. "That's well done. I didn't know anyone round here could."

"I did it. I took a course in commercial art in high school, but my heart was in the land."

"Like mine," said Madeleine.

It had been a good idea to tell him in front of someone else. He hadn't bawled her out.

But he did say quietly, "This is all very well, but you'll kill yourself, Lindsay. You can't run this single handed."

"I think I should be able to get part-time help. Mrs. Linmuir's daughter would like a part-time job, but doesn't like housework. That is if the volume of business merits a helper. Not that I've said anything yet, but I was at Linmuirs' the other day and the mother said she did wish they were nearer Alex as Jenny'd love a job in a milkbar. They need her help on the farm, part-time." She turned to Euan, "You won't raise any objections, will you?"

His face set. "Lot of good my doing so now, don't you think? I might have appreciated being asked earlier."

"Here we go," said Madeleine irrepressibly. "We're going to be right in the middle of a donnybrook any moment."

Euan ignored her. "Why *didn't* you discuss it with me, Lindsay?"

Madeleine said, "My dear man, because she knew you'd give the thumbs down sign, of course."

Lindsay saw Euan's lip tighten. "Why? I might have enjoyed helping. No wonder she's been looking pale and tired. And thinner. Talk about independent! I've taken all sorts of aid from you, Lindsay, but you're stiff necked with pride when it comes to letting me return it."

"That isn't true. You were responsible for my being given this place. I accepted that. I can't be too beholden to you . . . and I was afraid you'd put a spoke in my wheel."

Euan snorted.

Madeleine laughed again. "What did I tell you? Here we go again. Jock's in one of his rare rages."

"I am *not* angry, Madeleine. I — "

"Oh, la, la! No, of course you aren't angry . . . you only look as if you'd like to bite a nail in half, my sweet."

He ignored her and spoke to Lindsay. "What made you think I'd put a spoke in your wheel? I'm not the wet blanket type. I admire industry. I admire independence, but I also like people to be open and above board. How can you — "

"You know perfectly well it's just that we see things differently. That we don't exactly see eye to eye on — "

Madeleine gave way to real mirth. "Now, I'd have thought you did. If you remember, when I came in, if you weren't eye to eye you were certainly lip to — "

Euan's hand came down heavily on her shoulder. "That'll do, Madeleine. You ought to have gone away, not come in."

Madeleine looked up at him, narrowed her eyes. "Jock, you really are angry. You're serious. You're out and out mad because I came in just then. That means — "

It was too much for Lindsay. She'd had more than enough of Euan's playacting. She turned to Madeleine furious. "It didn't mean a thing," she snapped. "I'll tell you why he kissed me . . . because he must have seen you pass the window. *Because he's just trying to make you jealous. Because he and your mother are in cahoots together.* That's why!"

Euan swung around, gave an incredulous look at Lindsay, strode to the door, went without a word while the slam of the door reverberated through the house.

Lindsay and Madeleine were left staring at each other. Finally Madeleine said uncertainly, unhappily, "Lindsay, you weren't struggling. I thought . . . "

"Of course you'd think I was submitting willingly. I had a full bottle of mercuro-chrome in my hands and a good dress on. I wish I'd poured it all over him!"

"Oh, dear, what a mix-up. It's this darned contrary streak in me. I know my faults, believe me. The more mother pushes me towards Jock, the more I rebel. You'd think she'd know. Lindsay, I'd better go and make my peace with him. We've never had a serious quarrel in our lives. He's the only person I don't fight with." She seized Lindsay, kissed her, said, "Don't lose any sleep over it, pet, it will all come out in the wash. I think your idea's grand. If Jenny won't take it on, I will. Bless you, darling, you've made me see things differently. I'll drive up to the homestead, I'll be there by the time he gets there."

During the night, as she tossed restlessly, Lindsay asked herself why she felt so utterly miserable. She found the answer, too.

It was ridiculous. It was unthinkable. But it was true.

She loved Euan Hazeldean, who only used her to bring the girl he wanted to marry to the point of accepting him. And she despised herself because it was more than foolish to love a man she could not trust. A man who was so callous that he had no word of censure for a man who had left a blind woman to bear his baby, left her alone and in darkness. Even Neill had seen things clearer than that, had tried to make amends. Even Euan's love for Madeleine wasn't disinterested. She would inherit the adjoining estate, so even if he should fail to get Rhoslochan into his hands, he would at least, in time, become a landowner here. It had been clever to try to soften her by deeding her the Accommodation House, but at least she had seen through that . . .

7

H E was reserved and distant with her for a few days, something that made him maddeningly punctilous. He consulted her about various aspects of the new venture, sent Mick up with the tractor and the two of them removed a macrocarpa he thought might be a parking hazard; he brought up the lawn mower and mowed the grass outside the Accommodation House. He even asked her if she had enough money to pay for all she had ordered.

Mrs. Ford was as enthusiastic as Madeleine, and said so in her usual torrent of words. She had a heart of gold, brought over some of their relics of the mining days for the museum, baked her a huge stock of shortbread.

"It'll keep, love, perhaps see you through the first week if you get the customers I think you will. How about getting some of those gigantic bobbins from the Hydro Company — the ones they wind cable on — for outside tables. Paint them all colors. Then, if you run short of room, you could serve afternoon tea outside. Better stock up with chocolates and sweets and paperbacks. People going camping always forget something to read. And ice cream."

"I can't afford to spend anything on refrigerators," Lindsay told her.

"Oh, I think the firms would supply them. I'll find out. After all, my brother owns an ice-cream factory in Dunedin. I'll fix it so he gets everything you need." She was as good as her word.

But Madeleine put her foot down when her mother wanted to come and serve in the shop. "No, pet. You'd talk their heads off — people like to pop in and be on their way. Besides, this is Lindsay's show. You're a wonderful organizer, I know, but the one trouble with organizers is that they overshadow other people, don't let them develop their own potentiality. I mean it. In fact, my darling mother, what you've never yet realized is that I'm quite capable of running my own life."

Lindsay was amazed to find Mrs. Ford showed no resentment, even looked delighted. She felt strangely detached from things. Her mind would wander back to that night. If only Madeleine hadn't come in just then! *But that was the only reason he kissed you, you idiot*, she reminded herself savagely.

To bolster up her spirits she kept telling herself it was just as well. She might have given herself away. And with a man like Euan Hazeldean that would be disastrous. Better to keep your feelings in check, lest you lose sight of the fact that he was up to no good. She forced herself to dwell on what she knew of him: the way he wouldn't let her phone the lawyer on arrival; the day she had passed the little office in the homestead and had heard him say, 'I hear Lindsay coming. Better hang up now. Goodbye, Jim.' When she had been here six months she would ask to see the figures of the estate. She ought to know where the twins stood. They had all their lives ahead of them, their education.

She got another letter from Nessie Lockhart, Robin's brother's wife.

Alastair's mind is made up now. He thinks that for the boys' sakes we ought to get away from here. He's always been set on New Zealand. He's applied for tickets. In fact, he had long before without telling me. If you know of any farmer wanting a married couple, we're the ones! It would be grand to be near you.

It could be that the Linmuirs were the answer to that. Lindsay spent quite a bit of time over there. It was so relaxing — nobody schemed, there were no tensions. Alec Linmuir had come from very near Feadan when he was just a lad. Douglas helped his father on the farm but wanted a couple of years at Lincoln College.

"I very much want him to do just that, Lindsay," said Alec. "But I'll have to have a man. He's not going till the year after this, but anyway. I'd like him to have a bit of outside experience before he comes back. Jock Hazeldean did. First at Lincoln, then up in the high country. Theory and practice, they're aye the thing to pair. And it certainly paid dividends with Rhoslochan. Jock's a grand farmer. His run is the best in the district now."

His run. Well, to all intents and purposes it was.

She said, "Alec, I've friends back home — Feadan — who would like to come out. In fact their reservations are made for next year. Alastair is a wonderful farmer and shepherd, and almost as good as a vet. Nessie, his wife, is a grand cook come shearing and harvest. They'll be here September. They told me to look up advertisements for them, about then. They want Otago." She grinned. "They still want to reside over the border, you see."

Alec Linmuir leaped at it. "Give me their address, lassie. I'll write them this verra night. September, eh? Time Doug goes to Canterbury. There's a good house standing empty. We'd a married couple when the children were wee."

The twins and Neill were most enthusiastic about the tea shop. They helped Lindsay finish the decorating. Mick came down evenings and painted the outside woodwork. Euan, rather more taciturn than usual — because she'd spiked his guns with Madeleine, she supposed — brought in a hired sander and evened out the floor of the old bar.

"You don't get timber like this today, or workmanship, either," he declared.

On his heels came Mrs. Ford with an electric floor polisher. Lindsay protested. "I can't take that, Fordsy. It's sweet of you, but they are so expensive."

"Nonsense, girl, I've not bought it specially. It's that daft family of mine — the menfolk, I mean — who are so keen on mechanical gadgets they can't turn a traveler away. The things I've got I can't — won't — use! All I have to polish is one small passage near the upstairs bathroom — the rest of the floors are plasticized — and they buy me this! I can't bear having to plug it in. I just grab a tin of wax polish and a couple of dustcloths and it's done. But if I give it to you they'll stop moaning about wasting the thing. You can't hope to keep on polishing this by hand. Besides, I owe you a present. For helping the situation along with Madeleine. It's coming on very nicely.

I can read the signs. Madeleine is very restless."

Lindsay realized it was true enough. Euan was only dour with herself. He and Madeleine were together much more now, going round the sheep, talking stock and markets, fertilizers, aerial top dressing of the hill pastures, shearing, immunizing.

Madeleine didn't only have beauty, she had brains too.

It was impossible to stem Fordsy's gifts or ideas. She made excursions far back into the bush for trailing creepers, logs and ferns, and, blissfully happy, transplanted them in the grove behind the Accommodation House. She got her long-suffering husband to bring down two garden seats she vowed she wanted to get rid of and set up white garden pegs with the names of the various trees and ferns and subalpine plants that flourished beneath her fingers.

"Just the thing to interest the overseas tourists, Lindsay. Mark my words. Half of them don't want to go to the inaccessible places to see them. Here they can do it in comfort, two minutes from the main road. I've always wanted to do something like this. I got Euan to do the lettering. Isn't it fortunate that there are so many native trees in this glade? We tend to get mostly English ones round our homesteads. Noticed that? I've blended both at Westeringhill. Gives such contrast in autumn. Ever think New Zealand couldn't have been half so beautiful till the pioneers arrived? No true autumn. But now the golds and russets clash so magnificently with the evergreens. That's a good sentence, don't you think? I've often wished I could write half as well as I talk. You're a good listener, Lindsay. The family doesn't listen to half I say. Now what would you like me to do next? Polish the silver?

"Oh, by the way, you ought to have a sign up each side of here to approaching motorists. You know . . . Macrae's Scottish Tearoom in half a mile. I'll ring my husband and tell him to get cracking on whoever has the authority. It'll come better from him, you know, an old resident. And, Madeleine, what do you think about having our old swing brought down? Those chains are as good as new. I'll get Euan to put it under those pines. Great attraction for youngsters. Parents like to sit over their cuppas in peace." She went off to phone.

Lindsay looked helplessly at Madeleine. Madeleine laughed. "Might as well try to stop the Clutha coming through the gorge, my sweet! Just let her. Besides, this is a godsend, she's letting up on Euan and me a bit."

Lindsay's mind said to Lindsay's heart, *Only because she knows her dream is coming true at last.*

As the time of the opening drew near she began to feel nervous. What if car after car pased by and did not stop? Yet she must rise early to bake her scones and pancakes, oatcakes and bannocks — they must be fresh. How fortunate that the season was early this year and she had been able to make redcurrant jelly. Nothing like it with oatcakes. Later she'd make rowan and elderberry jelly.

"That should be most popular," said Mrs. Ford. "It's an odd thing, but very few New Zealand tearooms serve dishes of jam or jelly. My mother was

English and always felt it a lack. You get sandwiches and cakes and scones, but the scones are always just buttered. A few places do them with jam and cream, Devonshire-like, that's all. You know old Mrs. Ffoulkes in the wee cottage two miles on? I was thinking you could put a bit of earning power in her way. She's a great old body for jam making. She just lives on her pension, you know, so hasn't much to spare for charities. You know what a country this is for efforts for this and that . . . and so it should be, a land flowing with milk and honey . . . Well, she makes her jam. It sells like fun. She has that old orchard at the back of her, gone to seed a bit but produces wonderful fruit, notwithstanding. Makes the orchardists hopping mad that everywhere else can be frosted, but never Mrs. Ffoulkes' fruit. It's so sheltered. She could make jam and you could sell it. Campers never bring enough jam to last them, and Central Otago camps gets crowded . . . it's the climate, sun, sun and more sun. Motels going up everywhere . . . they'll need jam too." She stopped as an idea hit her.

"Lindsay, later on, that would be the thing. There's plenty of room — a couple of acres, aren't there? Besides, Euan would let you have more. When you've got a bit behind you, get a loan and build some motels. No meals to provide. Some give a Continental breakfast, but most cook their own. All you do is launder the linen and clean out the motels between guests. I — "

Madeleine got off the table she was sitting on. "No, you don't, mother. Leave Lindsay alone. Off you go and call dad with that message I gave you from Euan."

Laughing, Mrs. Ford disappeared.

Madeleine pulled a face. Lindsay burst out laughing. "It's all right, Madeleine, She's a darling. So goodhearted."

Madeleine signed. "I know. I love her dearly, but being good-hearted isn't quite enough. She needs restraint. I don't want to excuse myself, of course, but I'm sure that's why I've got this contrary streak in me. Mother organized me so much as a child. I got sort of dogged. I'll have to root it out of me when I get married, I can see that. It's funny, dad likes it.

He just goes serenely on, being proud of her. He adores her. So do I, but I wish she wouldn't rush in where angels fear to tread. I can think my own way through. It's such a silly business about Euan and me. If only she'd leave us alone. But what's the use! I bet the first thing I see when I get to heaven will be my darling mama rushing about with hobnailed boots on.

"And she's promised not to keep popping in when you've got customers. I'll give you a hand the first week — what a pity Jenny's still away. Still, you wouldn't want to be paying wages the first week."

"I mightn't want to any week," said Lindsay, beginning to suffer from cold feet.

★ ★ ★

She need not have worried: the tide of tourist traffic was setting in. Their first customers came at nine o'clock, having spent the night in Roxburgh. They feasted royally and were told no charge as they were the first to patronize them.

"There goes our first advertisement," said Madeleine happily. "Nothing like satisfied customers and word of mouth. Did you note that what pleased them most was they're North Islanders and it seemed fitting to them that in a Scottish province they should be served oatcakes and griddle cakes. They'll mention it to their fellow guests in Queenstown, who will all call on their way home."

They were so busy after that that they were exceedingly glad of a spell between lunch and afternoon teatime. Madeleine decided to slip home. "I'm expecting some important mail," she explained.

Madeleine had a flushed, starry-eyed look. Was it from the artist?

A few moments later Lindsay saw quite a crowd approaching . . . on foot. Where could they have come from? They were a motley lot, about nine of them, and in very casual clothes. Slightly arty, she thought.

One voice said, "Well, Rudy, I'll hand it to you that you certainly know where to break down. I'm starving."

They trooped in. The one called Rudy said, "Have you a phone? And would you know about garages? We've had a breakdown and it's most important we get to Queenstown tonight, though how, I don't know. The darned axle's gone. It'll take time. Is there a local garage, or will it have to be Alexandra?"

"I'll call Rhoslochan, the homestead. The manager will know," said Lindsay. "I've not been here long enough to know much about the garage at Crannog."

Euan said he'd call and find out. He arrived down in the station wagon a few minutes later. "You're out of luck with the local garage," he said. "Their breakdown outfit is out. Chap had an argument with a bridge in the back country. No one hurt, fortunately, but the car's down the bank and it will take ages. I've got someone coming from Alexandra."

In talking, he discovered they were a film unit doing tourist publicity stuff and had appointments in Queenstown.

Nevertheless Lindsay was surprised to hear Euan say, "It's bound to be a long job, so how about my lending you our station wagon and you can have the use of it? I'll pick up yours when its finished and then you can exchange mine for it when you come back."

Talk about casual New Zealanders. Still more casual was the acceptance. No more than, "How will you be for transport for yourself . . . ? Oh, well, if you can manage with the truck for a day or so, we'd certainly appreciate the loan of the wagon. It's our gear — we'd never get it into a small hired car. Thanks."

He paused, cast an eye around, began commenting on the interior. He went across to examine the gold-mining souvenirs, listened intently as Euan explained the history of the place, made a snap decision.

"We're on a project to encourage tourism. Eating places and so on haven't been New Zealand's best points — though we're getting on to it now. This is unusual enough to be included. How about us taking a few shots here and now — when you bring the station wagon down. We could pack our gear into it and bring it down here. We could include you and Miss Macrae in it. Let's have a look at the jail cell, if you don't mind."

Lindsay looked staggered. Euan said

to her in an aside, "Buck up . . . this is the finest ad you could possibly have. It will really put you on the map, here and overseas. Don't you realize you're about to star in a technicolor film!"

She revived. This was just the sort of crazy small country where things like this did happen. But she hissed at Euan, "Get Madeleine down. She'd be a whizz on technicolor with her coloring."

"Don't be daft — they'll want the owner."

Madeleine did come back, and was shot serving customers, who were also enchanted to figure in the publicity, however, Lindsay was the prime figure.

"You're just right," said Rudy, "and talking with that faint Scots accent makes it. We aim to stress Otago as the Caledonia of the Southern Hemisphere. We want a strong haggis-Burns-tartan flavor. And Mr. Hazeldean here can provide the pioneer link, talking of his ancestors and the gold-mining days."

Suddenly it was glorious fun and a good omen for the opening day. One of the publicity men decided he would write it up for one of the Dunedin papers. "You'll get quick results that way — it will be months before this is being shown, of course. It'll benefit you more next year, but an article in the *Star* would boost you now . . . No, I'd love to do it, it's a small return for the loan of the car."

By the time they left Lindsay had a slightly unreal feeling, as if she had dreamed the whole thing.

"Mother will be thrilled," said Madeleine, "but furious she missed it. But wasn't it a good thing she wasn't here. She'd have played the comic lead and not known it!"

★ ★ ★

The tea shop was a great success. The summer was a perfect one for holidaymakers, the shearing and haymaking over the whole province was uncomplicated by rain, the hills turned yellow and they were thankful for every bit of irrigation.

Hitchhikers streamed past, dusty, sunburned, burdened, glad of a respite and plain Scots fare; cars with trailers and caravans took to the roads as soon as the schools closed down. Jenny Linmuir came full-time to work, with her mother quite happy to forgo her help in the house since it meant that now Jenny wouldn't want to leave home.

Madeleine relieved Lindsay for an hour or two some days, sending her off to the Hazel Burn with the three children, bathing, on the hottest days. She even insisted that Lindsay take an hour and a half off from one-thirty on Christmas Day.

"It's no use protesting, Lindsay. Mother has organized it. We're having our dinner at twelve. She's cooking another for you and the kids at one-thirty. She says no one is going to spend all Christmas Day serving snacks to the traveling public and that Jenny and I can manage for a wee while."

It didn't seem possible that this could be Christmas, with the wheat turning gold in the paddocks, the gardens a riot of roses, bathing suits on the clotheslines every day, carols sung by young people in open-necked shirts and sunsuits, traveling around in open trucks in the long hot evenings.

And despite the temperatures they all cooked traditional Christmas dinners, made huge plum puddings and mince pies. Lindsay cooked small ones for sale to the campers. She insisted on providing the geese for Mrs. Ford's double dinner.

Euan, she supposed, would be at the first dinner. He wasn't. He appeared in the Holden to take her up, the children, freshly scrubbed, with shining, anticipatory faces beside him, Neill was driving.

"I thought you'd have had it with the Fords — and Madeleine," she said pointedly.

He shook his head. "Mrs. Ford believes in families being all together on Christmas Day."

"I'm not family," said Lindsay.

"Well, a clan connection, then," he said lazily. "Kith if not kin. All belonging to the homestead."

He'd been much more friendly since the tearoom opened. It was probably because they were both so busy and

231

hadn't had time to voice their mutual distrust so much. Besides, he'd been out a lot with Madeleine, she knew.

Lindsay thought she ought to be content with the success of her venture. It meant something to have such security, such a way of earning a living. It was hard work but satisfying. But at times she longed for something more . . . she was aware of a deep emotional lack, longed to be outside more in this exciting, hot, pulsating world.

Once the New Year holidays were over, Madeleine didn't come to the shop so much, but could be seen constantly at Rhoslochan, riding around the sheep with Euan often, but more often still, busying herself inside Rhoslochan, keeping its loveliness in order, settling down, as her mother said, to domesticity.

"It's all very fine for Madeleine to love the outdoor work more, but once you get married and a family comes along, you can't do it. And whoever you marry you need to be a housewife."

Madeleine merely said lightly, "Now you've got Jenny full-time you don't need me, and Euan says you'll kill yourself if you try to run the homestead, too, so I'm taking it on. So he won't continue to come down to you for lunch. I'll make it for him up there."

Lindsay had known a constriction of the heart. So she wouldn't see him every lunch hour now, even if sometimes she'd been so busy, he'd merely eaten at one of the little tables while she served. And she had so loved Rhoslochan. She had brought it up out of neglect to the charm of a house that was loved and cosseted.

Arrangements were well ahead now for Alastair and Nessie Lockhart and their family to come out in September. Robin had written twice more, in the same strain. The first Lindsay had answered curtly. She told him no, she wasn't likely to change her mind, did not answer his queries about the estate. She asked him not to write again.

The next letter she simply re-enclosed, unopened, in an airmail envelope and mailed it back to him.

So when, collecting the mail, she saw another letter with the Feadan postmark on it, she sighed. Alastair's letters were not mailed there, he lived ten miles away.

But it wasn't Robin's writing — in fact it looked like a woman's — and it wasn't addressed to her, anyway, but to Euan Hazeldean.

How strange.

A little apprehensively she took the mail up to Rhoslochan. Jenny was looking after the shop and the mail had been late.

The air was mild; little breezes blew caressingly against her hot temples, laden with summer perfumes drifting from the garden on the slight rise above her.

She was lucky. Neill and the children were away up the hill, their happy voices floating on the air. Mick could be seen on the roof of his house, painting it, and Wynne was sitting outside her door, her youngest boy in her lap. So Euan would be alone.

She caught herself up on the thought. What could that matter to her?

She tapped and went in. Euan was sitting at the big dining table, reading a whodunit. He looked relaxed, easy. He smiled at her in a way that made her heart turn over. Foolish, because it meant nothing. Only that he had such a dark, stern face that any smile lit it up.

It didn't mean he was particularly glad to see you.

"Oh, the mail's come at last. Sit down, Lindsay, everyone's out, and I'll glance through my mail. Not very exciting . . . mostly window envelopes." He slit them open, put the bills and receipts neatly together, anchored them with his pipe.

Lindsay had sat down on the window seat near the open window.

She said, as he slit the letter open, "I noticed that postmark . . . Feadan. Isn't that odd? Who in Feadan could be writing to you?"

"Mmm. Does seem odd. Let's see . . . " he drew out several sheets, looked at the back page. His brow smoothed out. "Oh, nothing but a coincidence. It's from our minister's wife. As you know the minister we've got at present is just on short-term supply. Mr. and Mrs. Abernethy are having a year in Europe. She must have just passed through Feadan and mailed it there. It isn't written from there."

Lindsay felt unaccountably relieved. "That's so. It's a tiny place, not much visited by tourists."

She waited, expecting him to pass on some snippet of news as he read. He didn't. She saw him stiffen, frown, shift his postion, read on. He read it right through, went to speak, changed his mind and went back to the beginning.

Lindsay stood up quietly, slipped out of the French windows, went down the rough stone steps Helen Hazeldean had set everywhere to tempt feet to stray through her lovely garden, went down to the far gate and walked towards the little lochan, reflecting back the rose and flame and gold and coral of the sunset.

The perfume of the bruised thyme came up to her, but she noticed it not. She was conscious of deep unease. She stood a long time by the lake edge, noticing only superficially the blue and green flight of the kingfisher, the darting grace of dragonflies over the surface, the reeds stirring. She flung stones in absently, watched the ripples widen and widen. Finally she found a huge flat rock and sat down.

It must have been a quarter of an hour later that she heard a step behind her on the shingle. She turned. Euan.

The light of the sunset was behind him, so she could not see his face well. The last rays fell squarely on her own upturned face.

"Lindsay?"

"Yes, Euan?"

"This Robin Lockhart?"

Her heart thudded against her side. What —

But she said steadily, "Yes . . . what about him?"

"I once asked you if you still loved him, and you wouldn't give me an answer. Remember?"

"Yes, Euan, I remember." She stood up, faced him.

He bent down a little, picked up her left hand, looked at it closely. "I noticed it once before. That paler strip around that finger. I wondered a little. That was where you wore Robin Lockharts' ring, was it?"

"Yes, but does it — "

"Does it concern me, you were going to say. As you said once before. Never mind. Be as secretive as you like. What could it matter to me?"

He turned and made his way back to the house, slowly and deliberately.

★ ★ ★

When he reached the house he drew the letter out of his pocket, smoothed it out, read it again. Well, it was best to know, at that.

It said:

Euan,

I feel a gossip, handing this on, yet I feel I should. Mrs. Ford wrote and told me about Neill's half sister and brother turning up. I was no more than mildly interested in what was rather a romantic tale and hadn't any idea where they came from in Scotland, of course.

But I was asked to give a talk on New Zealand at an institute meeting in the next village and some of the Feadan women were there. I did notice one battle-ax of a woman. I wasn't introduced, but later, sitting in my hostess's car waiting for her, I saw this woman in another car, also waiting for the driver. And the one who had presided over the meeting came and spoke to her.

I couldn't help overhearing. This woman called the battle-ax Lockhart and said how pleased she was she'd been able to come. Mrs. Lockhart said, 'Well, it was because she was speaking on New Zealand. My son's fiancée has not long gone out there. To Otago, too. She's been left a share in a very wealthy estate. I would like my son to go out there, too. Not for good, of course, but temporarily. To keep an eye on things, see she doesn't get cheated out of anything. It could be worth his while.'

I didn't become more than mildly interested in this, Euan, till the other woman said. 'Did your son's fiancée have a wealthy uncle or something over there?' and Mrs. Lockhart replied, 'No, a wealthy stepfather. Alexander Bairdmore. He married her mother, who had two children by him. They've all gone out.' Well, it's a mystery to me, Euan. I'll let you sift it out. Perhaps I didn't get the full strength of it, but I feel I at least owe it to you to put you on your guard. It smacked of acquisitiveness to me, and I'd not like to see you taken advantage of.

Now, having got that off my chest, and feeling really sneaky, I'll go on to something more pleasant. We've found it most interesting to meet up with the originals of so many of our Otago place-names, for instance yesterday . . .

Euan Hazeldean locked the letter away, went out and saddled Rosabelle . . .

8

LINDSAY thought wryly that at least she was so busy through the day that she was far too tired at nights to lie long and brood. She and Euan were outwardly polite to each other, no more. One thing she must do soon, and that was to ask the solicitor for a full statement about the estate. The trouble was she knew nothing about legal business and had no one to ask for advice.

Would it be best to go to another solicitor and ask him to make inquiries? It seemed the sensible thing to do. Nothing had been fully explained. Yet she shrank from the idea. She was the stranger. She was living on the bounty of Rhoslochan and making a decent living off it. What would a strange solicitor think?

The executors of Lex Bairdmore's estate — Jim MacWilson and Euan Hazeldean — had, merely on her own statement that her stepfather had promised her a legacy, deeded her the Accommodation House. They hadn't even asked to see the letter in which he had promised that.

She frowned. Wasn't that in itself suspicious? Had it been proffered a little too readily? Had they been eager to get her into a contented state? Was it meant to lull her suspicions?

When trade quietened down she must go to Dunedin on the bus one morning, stay overnight. Mrs. Linmuir would take the children.

Having decided that, she put all her energies into making the tea shop pay. It wasn't possible to get away from the tea shop except on Sundays. She did not open then. It was absolutely necessary to have one day with the children. After church, at Crannog they had a cold dinner, then usually all went off on the horses.

At first Euan had accompanied them, but not lately. He often went off on his own with Madeleine, or took her driving. The whole district seemed to be coupling them together now, inviting them out.

242

Today, for instance, they were visiting together in Alex.

It had been quieter in the shop. Mrs. Linmuir and Jenny had attended to the afternoon customers and told Lindsay to take the younger Linmuir children and the Bairdmores swimming in the little lochan. The children had thoroughly enjoyed it. Lindsay supposed she had too.

Wasn't it a little short of paradise to swim in that heavenly water under the cloudless sky, to come out, lie on sun-warmed rocks to dry, then, when you grew too hot, to plunge again? Wasn't this what she had wanted for the youngsters, a carefree healthy life? What more did she want?

Lying there, her head pillowed on her folded arms, her face hidden from the others, Lindsay answered that question honestly. She wanted a life of her own — the sort of things most women hungered for — the perfection and fulfilment of a man-woman world. A man's arms around you, his kisses on your lips, his the last voice to hear at night, the first voice to waken you in the morning. Not just an existence of working, sleeping, eating, but something to make you savor the full meaning of life.

It was still lonelier that night when the children went off to bed. She heard Euan's car rattle over the cattle stops at Westeringhill, taking Madeleine home. It was that kind of still, breathless night. He was a long time coming back, yet it was very late. It looked as if Euan wasn't cold-blooded anymore, as if he found it hard to say good-night . . . Lindsay got up restlessly, switched on the lights of the shop, prowled about, dusting the museum pieces. But everything reminded her of Euan. Especially the golden nugget gleaming in its tiny glass case. He had brought it down the day they opened, screwing it to the table. It had been found in Chophead Gully.

She must steel herself to hear any time of his engagement to Madeleine — the linking of two great estates — because no doubt he would continue on as manager of Rhoslochan till such time as Madeleine inherited Westeringhill.

What Helen Hazeldean and Ruth Ford

had planned long ago was coming to pass. Perhaps when Madeleine and Euan took over Westeringhill, he would transfer the sheep she was sure he was running here, on to that property.

She had discovered something only lately, something for sure.

The new Holden station wagon was registered in Euan Hazeldean's name.

He had taken her to Aledxandra and while waiting for him outside the stock and station agent's, he'd asked her to rub the windshield for him where several bees had flattened themselves out and left it smeared with honey. While fishing in the glove compartment for a dust rag, she had seen the insurance papers . . . in his name. It leaped up at her, the implication striking her like a blow, because she didn't want to believe these things about Euan.

Two days later, the papers were gone from the car.

He wasn't even bothering, these days, to pay her attention to spur Madeleine on. He didn't need to. She despised herself for the wistful thought.

She ought to hate Madeleine, but she

couldn't. Madeleine was so lighthearted, such fun, so gay and nonchalant, so generous with her time, so candid about herself.

She said, of her work at the tearoom, "Isn't it the oddest thing? I'd have thought I'd have found this penal servitude. Do you know, I washed dishes for a solid two hours on that busy Saturday and thought it fun. I'm discovering domesticated talents inside myself. When I do get married I'll be able to turn out batches of pikelets and oatcakes with the best of them. My dear mama thinks it's all your doing, Lindsay. She thinks it's love working a miracle. Come to that, I suppose it is. All a matter of wanting to and getting accustomed to it. At one time I hated everything that kept me from the stables. Well, honey, I'd better go, Euan is taking me out."

Lindsay wished she could go, too, somewhere, anywhere. But she was on duty. But tomorrow night she would take a long walk — go around the far side of the little lochan. Jenny would be on duty and would look after the children.

She found next night that walking did

do a lot to lift the weight of depression. As she passed the homestead, Rory, Euan's big golden Labrador, came out and joined her. She stopped and caressed his ears, happy to have his company.

They walked right around the lochan. Rory racing ahead of her, circling around, coming back. She came back to her favorite spot, the big flat rock by the weeping willow, though at first Rory had no intention of letting her sit and dream. He picked up sticks, dropped them at her feet, his forelegs braced in front of her, his attitude and his eyes beseeching her to throw them in the wee lake for him.

After twenty minutes of it Lindsay was exhausted and hot. Rory still pranced around. She shook her head, laughing. "No, Rory, you've worn me out. I'm a wreck!"

She kicked off her straw sandals, pulled up the wide skirt of her sunsuit, waded in. There was a splash as Rory landed in beside her, leaping from the rock, and completely showering her with spray.

Lindsay squealed, then laughed, the sound of merriment drifting uphill in the still summer air.

"You great idiot of a dog, Rory. Big, bumbling thing!"

He swam around madly.

Then they came out, Rory to shake himself, Lindsay to wring out the dripping skirt of her sunshine yellow sunsuit. She felt cooled and calmer. The breeze off the high tops, innocent now of a vestige of snow, played mildly on her bared shoulders. She heard footsteps coming down to the lochan. Foolish though it was, she instantly hoped it might be Euan. She didn't turn, she kept her eyes on Rory, lying panting. Rory wagged his tail, but that might mean it was only Mick, or Neill or — yes, it *was* Euan.

She looked up as he towered over her. Even the ends of her ponytail were wet. She was squeezing them out. She deftly twisted it into a less sophisticated version of her French twist, and thrust into it a comb that she took from her pocket.

She smiled up at him, uncertainly. His face was in shadow, for the setting sun was behind him, but she thought he looked grim.

"Cooling off, Euan?"

"I'm in need of it, certainly, but — "

he shrugged, let it go.

He didn't seem to notice how wet she was, to laughingly comment on it. He stood there, frowning.

Then he said, "I've just got back from Linmuir's."

Lindsay looked puzzled. He sounded accusing.

"Yes? Everyone all right? Jenny's at the tea shop. Is Jenny needed at home or something? If so I'll go back."

"No. Alex told me about your plan to get young Lockhart out here this year."

"Yes. September." She looked wary, scared. There was something here she didn't understand.

"Why wait so long? You'd think he'd be keen to get here sooner."

"There wasn't a ship available sooner."

"What about air?"

"It cost so much more. That's a consideration."

"What's the big idea in getting him out here, Lindsay?"

She blinded. "Euan, I don't have to consult *you* about such things, do I? It's a free country, isn't it?"

"It sure is, but I think you could be

more open about it."

She said nothing, completely puzzled.

He went on, "Why is he coming?"

"To better his position. Lots of men emigrate. A young country . . . plenty of chances."

His voice held the derisive note she so detested. "You mean plenty of pickings, don't you?"

Lindsay felt the hot anger burn up through her, clean to the roots of her hair. "I beg your pardon. He's coming out here to work, and *will* work. He's a wonderful worker."

"Bully for him! I still think he's after the pickings."

Her eyes met his. Hers too were greenish at the moment. "That makes me laugh . . . *coming from you*. Perhaps you think everyone is calculating like yourself, and acquisitive in regard to land. It's all you think about . . . more and more land."

He made an impatient gesture. "You're evading the issue. Why don't you tell me why you're bringing him out? I'm convinced there's a reason."

Lindsay's eyes blazed into his. "All

right, then. Perhaps I'm bringing him out to look after my interests. Mine and the children's. I feel I need someone of my own, someone I can trust."

The dark face darkend still more, the lines from mouth to chin deepened, his eyes narrowed. "It pays me to make you angry. We get the truth then. It still amazes me, how you can look so dewy eyed and innocent, so candid . . . and be so deep. Ach!"

He took an angry, threatening step towards her. Rory, lying at her feet, uttered a tiny growl, deep in his throat.

Euan Hazeldean looked absolutely amazed. He made a gesture towards the dog. "You've even hoodwinked my dog," he said bitterly.

Lindsay ignored that. "Let me tell you *I* didn't ask for the Accommodation House property. I only asked to rent it. *I'm* not after the pickings. And what the children get is their own . . . their father's. And my mother ought to have had more all those years ago!"

He started to say, "Your mother ought to have — " He cut himself off, turned on his heel, strode up the hill.

Lindsay watched him go, a hand to her mouth. "Go on, Rory," she said. "You'd better go with him. Off you go, boy."

Rory got up most uncertainly and followed Euan, his tail down.

★ ★ ★

Euan called her the next morning. "It's Hazeldean here. Don't bother to cook us an evening meal tonight. We shan't be coming down for it. We'll get our own."

Lindsay was determined her voice should not shake. "Very well, that will suit me fine. I really prefer to have my time for the shop. That's much more profitable *and* congenial. What will you give as a reason to Neill? Not that I'm really interested, but it's just as well to know since he's always in and out."

"I'll say I'm far too busy, that it cuts into too much time to be worth it."

"Neill might possibly think otherwise. He could still come."

"Neill will be quite happy. Madeleine will cook our meal. She's keen to learn the domestic ropes now."

"Oh, good show. Then I needn't worry whatever about Neill getting a good nourishing meal."

"Not at all." He hung up.

Lindsay hung up too, and two minutes later discovered she was staring at the phone, hands still clenched.

Why did he feel so strongly about Alastair Lockhart coming here? She didn't need Alastair to fight her battles, anyway. In fact the less he knew the better. She wanted no hint of any friction here to get back to Feadan . . . to Robin or his mother. It looked as if Euan Hazeldean didn't want any knowledgeable man here, asking questions on their behalf.

Neill always came in for a cup of coffee and a snack as he got off the school bus, but Lindsay decided to say nothing to him. That was over to that taciturn, inexplicable man up at Rhoslochan.

Yet it gave her a pang when Neill, in the old kitchen of the quarters, gave an appreciative sniff, went across to the stove, lifted a lid and said, "Ah, steak-and-kidney pudding! You know, sis, I like hot meals even in summer. You get a bit tired of cold mutton and salad. Boy, did we or did we not have too much of that when Aunt Helen went up to look after Bess's triplets! Wynne couldn't always manage to cook a dinner at her place and ours, so it used to be cold mutton and salad, countless times, *ad nauseam*."

Lindsay smiled mechanically, "Well, I'm very fond of salads myself, but I don't like a diet of cold meat all summer long."

"Been busy, Lindsay?" Neill inquired.

"Yes. And I had an inquiry from a firm running bus tours. That was for lunches, though, not mid-morning and afternoon tea. I think I'll give it a go. I'm thinking of serving dinners and lunches when winter comes. It wouldn't be too busy then and might get my hands in for doing the next summer."

"I wouldn't, sis. You'd never get a let up then. And I reckon Euan'd put his foot down."

"Euan would put his foot down! Neill, it wouldn't be anything to do with Euan."

He grinned. "That's what you think! He's the boss, you know. Besides, he'd only be scared you'd overdo it. You work too hard as it is."

Lindsay said shortly, "I'll be pleasing myself about it without consulting Euan. He's not *my* guardian, you know, Neill."

Neill looked at her with a shrewd grin beyond his years and said quite gently, "No, but whatever Euan does is for the best. Boy, has that man got a head on his shoulders!"

Lindsay sighed. "The trouble is, Euan is a legend around here. But me, I'm the independent type, too. Tell me, Neill, didn't your father ever find him a bit overbearing?"

"Good Lord, no, Lindsay. He was dad's mainstay. I don't know what dad would've done without him. Well, I better get up and get some of my chores done. See you later."

Lindsay hadn't the heart to tell him he'd not be down for dinner.

Therefore she was much surprised when Neill, at five-thirty, walked in, sat down. She was ladling the steak-and-kidney pudding on to their plates, and paused, gravy dripping from her spoon.

"Neill, Euan said you'd be having dinner up there from now on — that he was finding it a bind coming down here every night."

"Yes, so he said. I took one look at the table . . . cold mutton and beetroot . . . and said, 'Well, suit yourself, old boy, but I'm going down to have steak-and-kidney pie.'"

Lindsay said hesitantly, "Wasn't Madeleine there? Mightn't she be hurt? Neill, you're most welcome, of course, but — "

"But me no buts, sis. Euan did say pretty sharply, 'Neill, Madeleine came down especially to get this ready,' but I just grinned and said, 'Well, it could be a case of two's company, three's a crowd, so I'll leave you to it.'"

So Neill had summed up the situation, realized that some day Madeleine might be the manager's wife on Rhoslochan. Nevertheless Lindsay did not want Euan Hazeldean to think she was trying to wean Neill away.

Accordingly that night when she heard Madeleine's car sweep over the rattling cattle stops on her way home, she called the homestead.

She said stiffly, "I would like you to know, Euan, that I didn't invite Neill to have his dinner with us. But I couldn't say anything. I left it to you to explain. Perhaps you didn't do it very well. So I hope you're not angry."

His voice was derisive. "Of course I'm not angry. Didn't it mean I had Madeleine to myself?"

Lindsay bit her lip. Of course. Why on earth had she called?

She said coolly, "I quite realize that, of course, but you're so thrawn I thought you might want him there just to spite me."

"What a very charming opinion of me you seem to have!"

"Is that so very strange? I'm hardly likely to have a good one. If you're trying to freeze me out, Euan Hazeldean, you won't succeed. This attitude of yours — resentful of my having any of my own friends in Central Otago — I find ridiculous in the extreme. Neill is so delighted to have kin of his own here — he and Morag and Callum are quite inseparable — that I will not refuse to have him here, I will *not* hurt his feelings!"

"I'm not trying to drive a wedge between you and Neill. Neill can please himself where he has his dinner."

"That sounds most magnanimous. I think it's a pity that you took a stand like this at all. It divides Neill's loyalties, and that's something that shouldn't be done. For the children's sakes, because they've all three suffered bereavement this past year, I would have been willing to continue as we were, even to breaking bread with someone I detest! But apparently you weren't civilized enough to do that."

"I could have . . . had I thought it worth while. But Madeleine is a better aid to the digestion, I find. Better a dinner of herbs where love is, you know, than a steak-and-kidney pudding eaten with discord!"

Lindsay said furiously, "Are you finding something to laugh at in this? I'm not. I find it childish. You don't approve of someone from my old, dear, familiar world coming out here to New Zealand to share its advantages, so you'll no longer eat at my table."

His laugh was unpleasant. "Advantages, eh? I called them pickings last night. I still do. Lindsay, it's not your getting him out here that rankles, it's your secrecy, your underhandedness. Do you wonder I'd rather eat with Madeleine? Her only fault is a certain inability to make up her mind. At least she's as open as the day — a refreshing change!"

Lindsay drew in a deep breath to steady her temper, managed to say just as cuttingly, "I've no doubt at all that it would suit you very well, Euan, to have me open-mouthed, to tell you everything. But I'm no innocent, no pigeon for the plucking. And if I'm alone at the moment I'll soon have a man from my own land to stand behind me. I've never banged a receiver up in anyone's ear in my life, but I'm warning you I'm going to hang up right now. Goodbye!"

9

IT was almost incredible how little the children noticed, perhaps because it was so busy a time on the farm. The days were never long enough. Sometimes Lindsay was so tired she felt like dropping in her tracks, but her bank balance was growing and in the following year she might be able to get hold of another helper and take time off more regularly.

Neill said one day, laughing, "Euan's like a bear with a sore head this morning. I'm letting him cool off. I've finished my Saturday chores, so I've come to mow your lawns. Callum's been neglecting them a bit, hasn't he?"

"Yes, he's been so interested in this project at the school — writing up a history, very localized, of the gold days. So he's been out at everyone's places, seeing if they can dig up old records and souvenirs. Johnny Grant's been over sketching things in our museum — that child's a wonder at black-and-white

260

sketches — and Callum's discovered in himself quite a flair for writing.

"The only thing that worries me is that I'm not at all sure old Duncan Mackay isn't stringing him on a bit with the local legends. Callum spends hours down there. It's not that he's dodged the lawns, exactly, Neill, but that I said I'd do them, in the evenings, and then I haven't quite managed them. We've been busier than I expected. Good thing, I feel that given a couple of seasons like this I might be able to buy this place."

Neill stared. "Buy it? Are you mad, Lindsay? It was deeded to you."

Her voice was somber. "I know. But I have no real claim to it, and I hate being under an obligation."

Neil laughed. "A true Scot! But, Lindsay, I feel you deserve it. If my father married your mother he was responsible for you, too, surely. But poor old dad, he was so weak, he couldn't take responsibility. You don't owe this estate a thing."

"I can't look on it like that, Neill, but — " her eyes softened " — I do appreciate your saying that. You've never thought I came here just for — just for the pickings, did you, Neill?"

He gave a great shout of boyish laughter. "You ninny! Of course not. Who would? This is Callum's and Morag's home, same as mine. You had to come to look after them. If only Aunt Helen had been home, you wouldn't have needed to move down here at all. But Euan was afraid you'd get talked about. You would have too, I suppose."

He got up, bit thoughtfully into the last of the pikelets.

"Well, I'd better get cracking. By the time I've mowed the lawns old Euan might be in a better mood." He cocked a knowing eye at Lindsay. "He never used to be like this. Seemed able to take every setback in his stride. Not like dad. Reckon this place'd have gone out of the hands of the family long ago if it hadn't been for Euan. He somehow kept dad on the rails. Dad was bit too fond of the bottle and the dice, you know. But Euan'll be all right." He looked back over his shoulder, winked. "Must be love upsetting him. They say the true

262

sort never runs smoothly." He chuckled and was gone, and the next moment Lindsay heard the whirring of the lawn mower. She'd see that young Callum trimmed the edges, he mustn't rely too much on his brother, who had plenty to do up at the homestead. Besides, it might make Euan madder than ever.

One thing she decided . . . she wouldn't wait any longer to go to Dunedin and consult a solicitor. Euan Hazeldean had had things his own way too long. Lex Bairdmore had been irresponsible, fond of liquor, often in town . . . that had given the manager a chance to swing things his way, it must be looked into.

She walked into the shop. Jenny was wiping tables after some departing guests.

"Jenny, would there be any chance of your mother helping here on Monday to let me away on the early bus for Dunedin? I'd be back by night."

"What about Madeleine, Lindsay?"

Lindsay said slowly, "I'd rather not ask her. She and Wynne between them have been looking after the homestead and she does his evening meal now. You know what Mrs. Ford's like, so organizing.

She'd immediately, out of the kindness of her heart, offer to drive me in, and honestly I'd like a day by myself."

Jenny nodded. "I know. She's rather overpowering. If she discovered a sale on she'd drag you there for bargains whether you wanted them or not. Right. We'll say nothing to anyone. I'll warn mum not to let on even to Euan. He'd be bound to tell Madeleine."

★ ★ ★

As the bus traveled over the lovely miles between Crannog and Dunedin, Lindsay's spirits lifted a little. Perhaps she had just needed to get away from Rhoslochan and all its problems . . . from the sight of Euan riding around his paddocks with never a glance in the direction of the Accommodation House, taking his mail from the box, never bringing hers in . . . hearing the children prattle of him constantly. They were forever up at the big house, or around the outbuildings, and didn't seem to notice Euan was never down now.

Though Callum had said, "Sis, the

garden up at the homestead is pretty weedy, haven't you managed any gardening there lately?"

She'd snapped. "Of course not! I'm not a machine. I've this garden here to do. I got that homestead garden weed-perfect, and if those two up there can't keep it that way it's just too bad!"

She told herself she must try to get out more, to think less about the man she couldn't help but love, yet distrusted. She despised herself most of all for that. She looked back now at her girlhood years when she had sometimes wondered how her mother could have fallen prey to the facile charm of Lex Bairdmore, with more understanding.

It did you good, made you more tolerant, to realize your own judgment could be faulty. First she had fallen in love with Robin who had been no man to ride the water with, who had failed her at the first hint of trouble and had refused to be saddled with the twins. And now . . . now she was going to be strong, to turn her back on this new love. She would fight for the full rights of Neill and Morag and Callum because some day they would need their inheritance.

She had an idea it was being whittled down, that Euan Hazeldean's sheep were growing golden fleeces by grazing on Rhoslochan pastures, and he thought that with a girl as their guardian he was safe.

At the post office she looked up a business directory, pulled a face as she saw James MacWilson's name, and settled for Worleson and Pinberry.

She'd not thought it would be so hard to explain. She wasn't used to voicing suspicions of people, and even as she talked she became conscious of a sense of unreality that she could think Euan capable of cheating the estate. She told him all, of how her mother had gone blind before the birth of the children, how Lex Bairdmore had fled back to New Zealand.

Mr. Worleson said gravely, putting the tips of his fingers together, "I'm afraid that was typical of Alexander Bairdmore."

Lindsay looked astonished. "You knew him?"

"*Of* him. New Zealand is a small

country — in populations — and Dunedin is the capital of Otago and we are a particularly close-knit community. I'd not say that everybody knows everybody else, but the runs up there were few in number in the old days, and where a property has come down through four generations or so most local solicitors have a knowledge of the names, though in this case it went from the Hazeldeans to Bairdmore. That was a dastardly thing to do to your mother. Go on, Miss Macrae."

He began taking notes. The longer she talked the worse she felt, the more disloyal and degraded for even entertaining such suspicions. But that was stupid . . . she owed no loyalty to Euan.

She said finally, "Of course I could be utterly wrong, but it does seem to add up to something. Certain things have disarmed me — deeding me the property my shop is on, for instance — but I ask myself was it to allay my doubts. I've never seen any accounts of farm income, tax, or anything else, and surely, as the children's coguardian, I ought to have done."

"Yes, you ought. I think you were wise to set inquires afoot. I will say nothing more than that. If all is well, then your mind will be at rest. I will act on your behalf and insist on seeing all the necessary papers. The matter of the sheep, of course, possibly belonging to Hazeldean and being grazed on Rhoslochan, could be included in some form of agreement.

"I know Bairdmore had the name of being a man about town, therefore largely an absentee owner. It's possible there has been some fiddling. Euan Hazeldean might have persuaded himself that he was entitled to — er — profit himself as well as his owner, if he had done the major part of the work and kept the estate together. It may be a week or two before you hear from me. It must be conducted with the utmost delicacy, of course."

Lindsay thanked him, rose, said goodbye.

She was grateful for a little breeze blowing up from the harbor. She sat on a seat in Queen's Gardens for a while, to recover from her ordeal, from the feeling of sneakiness that possessd her, watching the pigeons feeding. She sat till many minutes and recordings of temperature had been flashed on the National Insurance Company's clock, lit against the deep blue of the sky over hills that even so near the city were girdled by belts of native bush.

Then, rested, she had a cup of coffee and plunged into an orgy of shopping. Nothing like fripperies to take your mind off unpleasantness, and besides, after all the years of pinching and scraping and making do, it was glorious to spend freely on oneself. She had earned every penny of this money by sheer hard work.

She even changed into a new suit, a fine lightweight crepe that was blue and green and lavender with a short jacket that buttoned all the way down the back and hung loosely over the tight skirt. She bought a swinging locket in black filigree on mother-of-pearl that represented, she noticed with amusement, King Bruce and the spider. She added new black gloves, high-heeled black shoes, a small hat, a bag.

"Oh," cried Jenny appreciatively, as the bus let Lindsay off. "Aren't you smart!

I'm so thrilled. Time you got yourself something new. I'm just about to close down. There's been no one in for the last half hour or so. I've got your tea ready . . . salmon mayonnaise. Mother said to tell you she's keeping Morag for the night. She had tea over home, and dad's rented a film — an underwater adventure, so they're having a night of it. Mum will cut her lunch with Bronwen's tomorrow and they can go off on the bus in the morning.

"Callum had tea there too and is off somewhere on that pony of his. What a rider that boy is! And isn't he keen on getting information about the gold days?"

Lindsay said anxiously, "He didn't go up Chophead Gully, did he? Euan stopped him going there alone. He's got some crazy idea of discovering what really happened in the gold-days' murder there. Euan found him searching for relics in a lot of loose shale and said it was far too dangerous, that once it starts to slip you can't stop it."

"Oh, if Euan forbade it, Callum wouldn't. I mean Euan's good with kids, but he doesn't stand any hanky-panky. One day last year — before you came — Bronwen and Sylvia West took the dinghy out on the little pink lake. Euan spotted them. He made them come in, walloped them both, rang their fathers and told them what he'd done. So I guess Callum's somewhere else, perhaps up at the homestead."

Lindsay nodded. It was hardly likely Callum would disobey.

But an hour later she was getting anxious. She rang the homestead and got no answer. They might all be outside; perhaps they had all gone boundary riding.

She called Wynne. Wynne said, "They're all away in Alexandra. At least Euan and Neill are — to the doctor. Neill got an outsized splinter in his wrist, off the jogger cart. Euan couldn't get it out, and thought it needed a local. And Mick's in for a Federated farmers' meeting in Crannog. Callum? I don't know, though I did see him on Peggotty a while back, heading for Chophead Gully. At least he was going that way. He wouldn't go up there on the pony, would he? I wonder if the others asked him to go round up the sheep in the valley past there. If so I suppose he's just forgotten the time. He'll come home when he's hungry."

"Yes, that's so. Cheerio for now, Wynne."

But when she had hung up she stayed quite still, her brow puckered. It wasn't like Callum. Morag had no idea of time, but Callum was so reliable, and he had a watch. What if he had decided to explore up the gully, knowing Euan was out? He'd tether the pony and explore on foot. He was so dead keen.

She didn't think she would wait any longer. She went to the window . . . the coral and flame of the sunset were giving place to the purples of dusk. She'd better hurry. A boy could sprain his ankle, fall down a bluff. He might have climbed the bed of the creek. It was almost dry, in these near-drought conditions. Anyway, she could check to see if the pony was there.

Alarm accelerated her pulses as her imagination got the better of her. She'd give Callum the length of her tongue if she found him safe and sound.

She unzipped her new skirt, slid out of it, shed her nylons, tugged off her lace half slip, pulled on her old green slacks. She didn't bother to change the top of the suit. She wanted to reach Chophead Gully while it was still light.

Thank goodness Dapple Dee was in the paddock and always so easily caught. She wasted no time. It was quite a ride to where the hills began to slope up from the paddocks. It was a well-defined track. You had to go past the Hazel Burn before you reached the gully. Just as Dapple Dee splashed through the waters of the burn, Callum's pony rounded the hill — riderless!

Lindsay reined up in absolute dismay. Callum had been thrown! Peggotty was heading straight for home as, tossing her head, she passed them with a speed that surprised Lindsay. She half wheeled, staring after the pony, then pulled herself together. Better not to go back. Wynne couldn't leave the children. Callum might not necessarily be in the gully, he might be just around the shoulder of the hill and perhaps only winded, or not even that. Just mad clean through that Peggotty had thrown him and bolted.

He'd had tumbles before and knew how to roll clear of the hooves. Lindsay dug her heels in and went for her life, rounding the shoulder of the hill with a prayer in her heart that she might see a small boy on foot.

No sign.

The track led to Chophead Gully and branched off to follow right onto a side road a couple of miles away. At the entrance to the gully she brought the pony to a stop and, cupping her hands, began calling.

No answer. It was more gloomy here. The trees clustered close and you had to pick your way carefully. Further up they thinned out, and about the higher parts of the creek were only *matagouri* and gnarled old *ngaio* trees leaning out from the bed. She took Dapple Dee carefully, stopping to listen often, calling, calling.

Where the ground began to climb in real earnest she dismounted, tethered Dapple Dee firmly, stood for along time calling.

Cold fear clutched her heart. Further

up were many evidences of the old-time mining — rough caves hollowed out for shelter, remnants of old sluices, pieces of rusted iron sticking up through the shingle. Callum must have gone up there. Usually he was as surefooted as a mountain goat. But he might not always avoid accident. He could be lying up there injured, perhaps knocked out, since he was not answering. Peggotty must have broken away, nervous at being left too long. Pray God, she found him and that he was not too badly injured.

She began climbing up the narrow gully where so many men, of so many nationalities, must have climbed before her, but she was seeking something far more precious than gold. She paused often to call.

Further up, the creek branched into two, only the main one with any water in it. The other one, running off left, had dark overhanging rocks and turned a bend so you could not see all the way up. That would be the one Euan had told them not to explore. There had been a small landslide there once, after deep snow had thawed and it wasn't safe, he had said. It was the very place Callum would want to rootle in to see if there were any relics.

"Here goes," said Lindsay, and began the ascent. Thank goodness there was no water; it was slippery enough.

Up and around the bend it opened up a little. Lindsay, her eyes searching frantically this way and that, saw an old tin pannikin half-buried in shingle. It hadn't been disturbed. Wouldn't Callum have fallen on it with cries of joy and unearthed it? Did it mean he had not come this way?

Another thought succeeded that. Callum was a thoughtful boy and given to method. He'd work out that there might be more, higher, and that it would be best not to burden oneself on the way up but collect it on the descent. So the fact that it was undisturbed needn't mean a thing.

She decided to go up and over those jutting rocks imbedded in the side of the narrowing gully. You'd get a good view from there. If there was no sign or sound of Callum then she would have to be sensible and go back, ride the pony to

Wynne's and raise the alarm. They could alert half a dozen people on the party line and it was just possible someone might have an idea where Callum was. The light wouldn't last much longer and she must be out of the gully before dark.

The last bit was rough going, but she certainly got a good view. Not that it availed her anything. She looked down . . . there was an easier way. A sheep track led down and around.

She wouldn't have to clamber down the bed of the stream that way. She found she was making better time . . . but then minutes later wished she'd kept to the other. The shadows were thicker here because the shoulder of the hill kept off the last rays of the sun. It was eerie and a little chilly now, and the grass was slippery. Must be a bit of drainage or seepage. Suddenly her left foot slipped. As she slid, she clutched a piece of *ngaio* twisting from the bank. It held for a moment, while she dangled. It was only a few feet to the bottom of the hollow, she judged, but she didn't want to sprain her ankle. She swung around a little to get a better hold, her feet scraping at the clay and shingle, felt the root give way and leaped.

She dropped, her feet struck something that wasn't rock at all, but wooden . . . and splintery . . . rotten.

It gave way with a crash, and Lindsay fell through, into a narrow pit, deep and slimy, with ferns reaching out to slap at her face with wet green fronds as she clutched wildly, screaming as she went, to land with an agonizing wrenching into watery slime and jagged rocks. She sank down, felt the cold, evil water come lapping over her shoulders and thought, fatalistically, This is it. My end. Will they ever find out what happened to me? And she lost consciousness.

★ ★ ★

How long she lay she did not know, but she woke to darkness, an almost tangible darkness. She lay there, soaked, chilled, in pain, partly submerged in the ooze, not knowing where she was at first, how she had got there. It was terrible to open your eyes and find no difference, no glimmer of light, to feel a damp blackness pressing on your eyeballs.

Remembrance came back to her with sickening impact. She was in Chophead Gully, down a mine shaft. A lot of the Chinese had drilled these, narrow, deep. She remembered Euan saying once, 'What patience they had, what courage, but it gives me claustrophobia to even think of it.' At the recollection panic rose in her, sheer, unadulterated panic. She screamed. At the sound of her own scream she was shocked into silence, there had been such terror in it.

On the heels of it came a realization that this wasn't as narrow as the ones she had heard described. It may have been to start with, but perhaps time had crumbled the walls away. How far had she fallen? Her legs, doubled under her, were resting on the bottom, and she was sure if she could stand that the water wouldn't reach much above her knees. The sides might not be completely perpendicular. She might, she just might be able to climb out if they were not too slippery. If only she could *see*!

Already, though, the darkness wasn't so thickly black. That meant her eyes were becoming accustomed to it. Suddenly her ears began drumming, her heart palpitating unpleasantly, every pressure point throbbing. Lindsay fought against it. If she were unconscious again she might sink beneath the ooze.

It stopped. She drew a shuddering breath of relief. She must keep panic at bay, try to take things calmly. First of all, draw in some good deep breaths.

She managed to maneuver herself on to her side, tried to force herself upright. A sharp pain stabbed at her side. She relaxed immediately, then, gently, and putting as little pressure as possible on that side, wriggled around. The pain came again, but not so badly. Her fingers, covered with slime, explored the area. Ah, she had broken, or cracked, a rib. Then she must be very careful. Though it was not as bad as a limb.

She lay, panting a little. If only she knew what time it was, how long she had lain, how soon they would miss her.

Her imagination ran riot. Jenny would have gone home. Morag was staying there for the night. Callum was lost, probably injured. Wynne might or might not phone to see if Callum were home. Mick would be late and Euan and Neill might have gone to the pictures in Alex after the splinter was out. But even if they came home early they weren't likely to call at the Accommodation House. She might not be missed till morning — till Jenny found the shop shut, the beds not slept in.

And where, where was Callum? At the thought that he, too, might be lying somewhere, injured, perhaps dead, the tears ran out of Lindsay's eyes. She pulled herself together. It didn't seem likely now that he was in Chophead Gully. If he had been thrown farther away, he'd be on one of the tracks, and more likely to be found when . . . if they were missed.

She began to hope that a considerable time had elapsed when she was knocked out. That might mean rescue was that much nearer. And in a moment she was going to try to get up.

This time she managed to stand. She reached up blindly. As far as she could reach there were only clay sides, running with moisture, ferns springing out, ferns that came away as she pulled.

Carefully, standing on one foot and swinging out the other in front of her, in case she suddenly plunged into deeper slime, she began exploring the bottom. That might give her an idea of how wide the pit was. She could not bend to the water with her hands because it hurt the rib. It was wider than she thought, quite six feet across. And at the other side was a ledge, just a foot or two above the water, but she could sit on it.

It wasn't big enough to get her feet on, they still had to rest on the bottom, but at least it kept her out of the stinking, chilling water for three quarters of her height. The fact that she had been able to help herself even a little gave her fresh courage. Perhaps, come daylight, she might be able to scrape away the walls to get a foothold . . . if the shaft wasn't too long. At the thought of being there all night she could have screamed again.

Her foot was resting on a rock, a round rock that would keep moving. If only it would stop wobbling, it would support her better, perhaps keep her legs farther out, though it seemed only big enough for one foot. Perhaps she could wedge it a bit.

It was light for a rock. Perhaps pumice . . . although she didn't think you got that in the south. Her toes explored it — she had lost her sandals somewhere. Goodness, how water-worn it was. Some holes went right through. Lindsay decided to bend on her uninjured side and wedge it. It was necessary to keep doing something. When she got a bit more secure she was going to yell her head off. She had more breath and strength now. Because help might be coming, and once they found Dapple Dee, they would know she was in the gully. She managed to get hold of the rock in one of the holes and lifted it. It didn't take half the effort she expected. What on earth was it? In the darkness her fingers explored it. Three holes and some sort of gash. Her fingers ran along the gash, encountered a row of ridges. She realized what it was and cast it from her, a scream of pure terror breaking from her and echoing madly in the hills. It was a skull.

Even as it splashed and sank she took

herself to task. It could be a sheep's head. But she knew it wasn't. At that moment she heard the terrifying whinnying of Dapple Dee and knew instant hope. Her terrible scream had startled the pony so much she was making a monstrous noise. *Oh, keep it up, Dapple,* she prayed, *keep it up.* The sound gradually subsided. Suddenly, straining up through the agonizing darkness, Lindsay saw a star blink out.

Never would she forget it. One little ray of light! Then it was fairly late. Help might be at hand. She might be missed soon. The trouble was it was all conditional upon that 'might.'

Lindsay began to call. It wasn't till she had called half a dozen times that she realized the name she was calling over and over was "Euan . . . Euan!"

Two or three times more Dapple whinnied. Lindsay wondered if she would break away, and knew not what to hope. If Dapple arrived back at the homestead, distressed, with broken tether, they might start searching earlier. On the other hand, if she was tied here, it would narrow the area. But she had tied her so firmly! She kept stopping calling to listen, but there were so many noises in the night, some horrible noises. One sounded as if a stoat had got a rabbit. There were still a few, very few rabbits back in the hills. There was the lonely booming of a bittern in some faraway swamp, the sound of an owl hooting as it hunted and the sinister sucking of the slime very time she moved her feet, and move them she must to keep the circulation going.

Still she called. Still it seemed to her that her voice was buried with her in this vault. That only the echo sounded back to mock her, that she would never escape from this prison, that all she would ever see of the lovely world outside was that one little star, that someday her skull, too, would be buried in the slime.

She thought she was dreaming when she heard the voices. She had imagined an answering call so often. But it came again.

"Lindsay . . . Lindsay! Keep calling . . . where are you?" Euan's voice.

She slipped off the ledge, stood up, trying to throw her voice farther. "I'm in a mine shaft. Be careful, Euan. Don't slip. I fell down a bank on to the cover. I'm in a shaft . . . don't fall, too. Oh, do be careful! Here . . . this way . . . be careful!"

Then a beam of light from a flashlight shone down, a blessed, wonderful, saving beam of light.

"My God!" said Euan, and it was a prayer, not a blasphemy.

His face and Mick's peered down on her.

Euan said quietly, "Lindsay, how much hurt are you?"

"Very little. I've cracked a rib, but no broken limbs. I must have struck my head falling down, because I was out of it for a while. My forehead is cut, but only superficially. It's stopped bleeding. It's nothing."

"You were out of it? Merciful heavens, you might have gone under. Well, at least we've found you."

"But Callum . . . Euan, he's lost. He's thrown. I — "

"Callum is safe, Lindsay, and in a rare state. He was at old Duncan's. Peggotty broke away and he had to walk home. There's no phone there. Did you meet the pony and fear the worst?"

"Yes. Just near here. I wasn't being foolhardy, Euan. I started to come back as soon as it grew too dusky."

"Of course. No one is likely to scold you."

The flashlight began to describe circles, sweeping the walls. Euan and Mick were both talking at once. Then Euan said, "We've got to get you out of here with a rope ladder. There's one in the woolshed, and we'll need quite a few men. We'll — "

Her voice rose in a shriek, "Don't leave me! Not alone — I — "

"Steady," said Euan's voice. "Mick will go back for help. Lindsay, tell me . . . that side slopes outward a bit, doesn't it, above where you're leaning? Is the bottom fairly firm? I mean does it slope away . . . get deeper?"

"No, Euan. Your feet sink into it, but it's reasonably firm. Why?"

"Because I'm coming down to you till Mick gets back."

Her reaction was instant. "No, you aren't. Oh, no, Euan! It's enough for one to be in this mess. As long as you stay there with the flashlight I'll be all right."

"I'm coming. No arguing. It wouldn't be any use. You might black out again. I'd rather be down with you if that happens."

"He's right, Lindsay," said Mick. "It's not more than about twelve feet — well, perhaps fifteen, to the bottom. I'll help him down. No, okay, I'll be careful. I'll break away some of this rotten wood first."

Lindsay felt sick with apprehension. But Mick had a shepherd's crook with him. He held it, so did Euan, gradually letting his hand slip down, lying flat against the sloping side, his toes digging in. Suddenly there was a splash as he landed beside her.

Her hands grasped him, steadied him as he floundered, then Mick was saying: "Right, I'll be off. It'll be at least three-quarters of an hour, I reckon. If I can do it under, I will."

Euan's arms came around Lindsay, held her against him, gently because of the injured rib, comforting, strong, masculine, warm. He put his head down on hers, his chin against her head, said, "Oh, Lindsay, Lindsay," brokenly, and held her close.

Then his hand lifted her chin, his thumb fitted into its faint cleft and then she felt his lips coming over her dirty, scratched face, feeling for her mouth, finding it.

His fingers caressed her neck, the lobes of her ears, stroked back the hair from her ears. Suddenly he laughed. "I wonder if anyone has ever kissed a woman at the bottom of a mine shaft before?"

But Lindsay put her hand up to his face, touched moisture that wasn't slime or blood and said wonderingly, "Euan . . . you're crying!"

He drew in a deep breath. "Yes, Lindsay, I'm crying. I'll never forget hearing you . . . then seeing you . . . down there in the darkness. Oh, Lindsay, Lindsay!"

Presently he pulled himself together, said, "Now, these injuries. That rib. Listen, darling, is it broken inward or outward?"

"Outward, I think, Euan." Was she dreaming, or had he really called her darling? "I think it would be hurting more if it were inward, wouldn't it?"

"Yes. But I'd better find out which it is if I can, because I don't want to do any damage when we get you out. If it's inwardly broken we'll have to be most careful. Have you got a blouse on you can pull up?"

Suddenly she giggled so that he was afraid she might be getting hysterical. But she said, "I've got the top of my new suit on . . . I just bought it today. The most expensive I've every bought in my life."

She could sense that he grinned back. "We'll buy you half a dozen. Oh, I see it's loose. Take the flashlight, will you? I won't let go of it till you have it firmly."

"I've got it, Euan." She pulled her top up above her waist, leaving her midriff bare.

His fingers gently felt her ribs. "Just there," she said, wincing.

"Mmm, outward. There's quite a lump, an angular one. Good show. Sorry if that sounds callous, but it's so much better than inward. Though I'd still be happier if we could bind it

290

in some way before we haul you out."

"How could we? We haven't got a thing."

"You wouldn't have a garter belt on? I mean, pulled up, the elastic would hold it firm."

"No, I took it off when I took my stockings off. But never mind, I'll be careful going up."

"It's in case you slip. And I'm scared in case the skin breaks and infection gets in. Look, I'll use my shirt. I won't tear it up but knot it at the sleeve. It'll hang down behind, but the length of sleeves and the width of the shoulders should make it go around twice."

She made no demur. It was a gray twill shirt, strong. It supported her fairly comfortably.

Euan said, "You've lost a shoe, I think. It seems to be bumping against my legs."

He felt her shake, was glad she could see the funny side, then heard her say calmly, "It's not my shoe, Euan, they're gone completely. They were only sandals. It's somebody's skull."

"What? How the — "

"After all," she said demurely, "This *is* Chophead Gully. Why so surprised? Won't Callum be pleased!"

Euan, still incredulous, bent down, fished around, came up with it, said, "Light, please."

And there it was, sitting on his hand, reminiscent of the graveyard scene in Hamlet, and above the eyes the bone cleft in two.

"Murder most foul," said Euan. "Alas, poor Yorick."

"I'm afraid I screamed horribly when I fished it up and realized what it was." She shuddered at the recollection. "I'm only being nonchalant now because you're here with me."

He said quickly, "Because *I'm* with you, or because *someone* is here with you?"

She was silent.

He said softly, which was probably absurd because there was no one near, "I asked you a question, Lindsay."

She didn't know what to answer. There was so much to be explained before she could admit to her feelings.

She said slowly, "Euan, don't you

think that's the sort of question to ask in . . . rather different circumstances?"

She felt his wet body shake against hers. "How right you are . . . not exactly a moonlight-and-roses setting, is it? All right, Lindsay, it can wait. For a time when there won't be slime and a pit, horrible smells and skulls floating about. A time when you won't have a cracked rib, Lindsay. But oh, if you only knew what I went through when I was picturing you lost in the bush, injured, perhaps worse . . . then you would think this was heaven. Yet what you must have endured. It must have been ghastly. We didn't know this old shaft was here. The other ones we do know, and have made them safe.

"I got back from Clyde," he went on. "Neill's in the hospital there. It was more than a splinter, it was a positive chunk of wood. I suspected that, though the end was sliver-thin — the end that showed. They managed it with a local, but thought he was better in the hospital for the night, though I did say he had a sister who would look after him — you. He'll be out tomorrow.

Poor Callum! When you weren't home he phoned Wynne, and when she said you'd probably gone to look for him he was nearly demented. Your pony whinnying gave us the clue."

"I started Dapple Dee off by my screaming. Euan, do you think the skeleton is here, too, under our feet in the ooze?"

"No. It's in the local history books that three bodies and two heads were found in the river all those years ago. A drunken brawl, I believe, after a bonanza strike. Lindsay, are your feet completely frozen?"

"Yes, but since you came the rest of me is warm."

His head was resting on top of her head; she felt rather than saw him smile.

"I can't even hold you as close as I'd like to because of that rib, but a good hot bath will fix you up, I hope. Mick will have got Wynne to call the doctor. Poor chap, he'll begin to wonder what goes on at Rhoslochan."

Lindsay knew he was making light of it for her sake, that he didn't want her dwelling too much on that horrible hour or two of consciousness, trapped in this foul pit. She shivered. He tightened his arms a little.

"I hear voices, Lindsay. It's nearly over, your ordeal." He paused, added, "We've lots of things to discuss. You'll be in no shape for them for a few days. I know you've thought things odd — at Rhoslochan. But it can be explained. It won't matter now. We'll be together. Always."

She nodded. "Yes. Plenty of time." She clung to his shoulders, turned her face against his. Her voice shook. "Euan, I ought to thank you for coming down here. It would have been enough just to have you at the top, knowing someone was there, but . . . to have you here with me, sharing the horror, the cold, the beastliness, was . . . oh, you'll never know what it meant after being alone. There aren't any words . . . " her voice trailed off.

"Then don't try to find them, sweetheart. There aren't any as you say. Sometimes we don't need words. This says it for us."

His lips came to hers, gently, felt them

stir beneath his, respond.

Suddenly she knew that all that had passed between them of bitterness and recrimination and suspicion didn't matter. It was false. He would explain it all. This, this was reality, a glorious reality. Being here in Euan Hazeldean's arms, hearing his voice, not derisive, not accusing, but tender, low, loving.

Euan Hazeldean wasn't a man to cheat the fatherless, to lie, to steal. He was the man to ride the water with. She wanted to laugh. How apt. He was here *in* the water, with her! Tomorrow she would write to Mr. Worleson, tell him her suspicions were unjust, that he need proceed no further with his inquiries. What a blessing he had said it would take time.

The voices were quite near now. Euan chuckled. "They'll think every moment has been torture . . . how little they know! Not that I won't be mighty relieved to get you out of here and into bed and a doctor in attendance. Hello there! Yes, we're all right. Cold and in a frightful mess, but all right."

Alex Linmuir was there, Rod Ford

and his hired man. They had an enormous lantern that was immeasurably comforting. Suddenly the height above them seemed less. It could have been so much deeper. The men found firm ground farther back, and as the rope ladder was longer than was needed, they pegged a whole length of it away from the crumbling edge. They broke off a lot more of the rotten wood. Then they were ready.

Mick was lying on his stomach, reaching down toward her, Rod Ford was holding his legs.

"Don't haul her over when she gets to the top," instructed Euan. "She's got a broken rib. Let her crawl slowly over it herself. Up you go, Lindsay."

He stood in the slime, held her steady. Even grasping the sides of the rope ladder made her gasp as it swung to and fro and squeezed her arms against her sides. But Euan held her firmly, reaching up as far as he could. She turned her head.

"Euan, you won't slip, will you? We don't know what's under that slime. Rocks could shift — and there's no one to hold it for you."

He grinned. "Up with you, lass, and I'll be right after you. Now that's as high as I can reach. About four rungs and Mick'll have you. Go on . . . that's it . . . steady? Give yourself a spell after each . . . Careful, Mick. Just steady her. Now get your breath and climb over. You can't slip now."

She crumpled for no more than a moment as she reached solid ground, then she turned, on her knees, to peer over.

"No, you don't," said Alec. "Back here with you. You might get giddy. Jock'll be right. He's a tough *hombre*, that one. Right, Jock."

Lindsay, crouched on the ground, saw Euan come over the top, get to his knees, and she keeled over. It was only momentary, due to the relief from strain, and she came to, to hear Alec Linmuir say, "Aye . . . what did I always say? A rare plucked 'un, is Lindsay Macrae. All the Macraes are."

They deemed it best to let her walk down the hill. Carrying her would put to much strain on the rib. Euan and Alec supported her. Her feet were so cold she couldn't feel the stones. Alec had put his socks on her, but they were still frozen. At the foot of the gully they had the truck, and it was all flat paddock to the house. They had a mattress on the tray of the truck, and blankets. Euan and Rod Ford sat beside her. Mick drove very gently.

She was aware that it was Rhoslochan they were taking her to. "Euan, I'd like to go home," she said.

He shook his head. "We want you right under our eye."

The doctor arrived as they did. Mrs. Linmuir was there, and a white-faced Jenny in tears. She mopped madly at her eyes so the doctor would let her stay.

"You can't attend to me like this," Lindsay said to the doctor. "I'm indescribable. I reek. I'm filthy!"

He laughed. "You don't have to tell me! But I must examine you first. Then if it won't do any further damage you can bath. If the rib is broken, I'll plaster you up after the bath. And what's all this about skulls? Really, what some people will do for the sake of their little tin-pot museums!"

Lindsay burst out laughing. "What do you think Euan did? He shoved it down his vest to climb up with! Callum, you can have it for the school museum. I will not have that thing grinning at me in the shop museum!"

After his examination the doctor decided a shower would be better than a bath. "And more hygienic . . . flow the filth away. Less risk to the rib. Not too hot. I'll have to have that wound on her forehead clean before I stitch it, but I don't want it opening up too much. Mrs. Linmuir, I want both you and Jenny to support her under the shower — you'll get splashed, but it can't be helped."

"As if that mattered!" they said in unison.

It was wonderful to feel clean again, to smell talcum powder instead of stench, to experience the matchless feel of warm pyjamas against one's skin.

The doctor injected a local, stitched her forehead, bound her ribs firmly, anointed her various scratches, and told her she had come off lucky.

Euan came in, also scrubbed clean, in dressing gown and pyjamas, and they all, including the doctor, had coffee. Then Jenny and Euan took her upstairs.

She went to go into the guest room she and Morag had used. Euan steered her past it. "You're going to the tower room — my mother's room. It's much more pleasant when you're going to be in bed a few days."

Lindsay looked alarmed. "But I'll just be walking wounded, won't I? People do walk around with broken ribs. There's the shop — "

"Doctor's orders. You'll have a reaction — shock. We're to guard against chill and excitement. Jenny is staying the night with you. I'll put a camp bed in for her. She and Madeleine will manage the shop between them, and Mrs. Linmuir is coming over every day till you're yourself again. I thought Fordsy would exhaust you too much. And the children will be all right. Morag will stay at Linmuir's and Callum can have his old sunporch back, here."

Lindsay gave in. They slipped her dressing gown off, an old one of Euan's mother's. They helped her into bed. She sank into it gratefully, warmth from the electric heating rising through to her.

Euan turned to Jenny. "Slip along to my room — you know it, I suppose? . . . and get the bedside clock. It's luminous, and if Lindsay is awake in the night she can see the time. It's very comforting if you can't sleep."

Lindsay knew without being told that it was because she had told him of the absolute horror of that suffocating darkness with no gleam of light, of the comfort of that one small star. And this was the man she had distrusted, struggled against loving . . . he turned swiftly as soon as Jenny was out of the room, bent and kissed her. "Good night, my love," he said, and was gone.

The sedative the doctor had given her was taking effect; she sank deeply into billowing clouds of sleep, in a dream of happiness.

10

THE next day she was one big ache, all bruises and sore places, but still content to lie and dream. She didn't see Euan alone at all, but that wouldn't matter, they had all the time in the world ahead of them.

Later she asked Mrs. Linmuir for pen and pad, but Mrs. Linmuir laughed at her. "No business letter is as urgent as all that, my dear. You just bide still. If it must go, get Jock to write it."

"Oh, no," said Lindsay hastily, "it's not as important as all that."

But Mrs. Linmuir had mentioned it to him. He came in with her when she brought Lindsay's lunch. "Some letter to do with the shop, Lindsay? Something urgent?"

She shook her head. "Not really. I didn't think I wouldn't be allowed to use a pen, and thought it would be another job out of the way, that's all."

"Well, you'd have to sit up to write,

and the doctor said you'd be better either lying or standing. Are you sure you wouldn't like me to write it? I could do it on the typewriter and you could just sign it."

"No, it can wait."

She decided she would get Jenny to smuggle a pad and ball-point pen in and ask her to mail it in their mailbox, not Rhoslochan's. Jenny wasn't overcurious, she might think Lindsay was being a little secretive, that's all. What a good thing inquiries would not be started yet. But she mustn't delay.

But she couldn't get Jenny alone. Perhaps she might after the shop shut down for the night. She'd say she must see Jenny about some sweet orders, and maybe they would leave them alone then. Euan just came up when Mrs. Linmuir did. He wasn't making the opportunity to be alone with her. He was probably thinking of what the doctor had said. The doctor came out in the afternoon and advised at least three more days in bed.

Poor Mrs. Linmuir had a busy time answering the phone as the news spread.

She switched some of the calls through to Lindsay, but not too many, and even those she warned not to talk too long. There was an extension on the table beside Euan's mother's bed.

In the late afternoon Lindsay decided she'd use it to ring Jenny at the shop. This could be a quieter time down there.

She had lifted the receiver when Euan's voice arrested her attention. Oh, she hadn't realized he was inside. She was about to replace it gently when what he said riveted the earpiece to her ear.

"She actually engaged a lawyer to look into things? Well, look, Jim, can you stall him off? Tell him you'll prepare a statement, but it will take a little time. Better appear very indignant on my behalf. Good Lord, I thought we'd bluffed it through very well, though there were times when it was a near thing. But for heaven's sake, don't let anything come out now. I want to get something clinched first — " he laughed " — and I've found a particularly ideal way of lulling her suspicions. Should be a hundred percent effective. No, you old son of a gun, I shan't tell you what — on a county exchange! I'll be able to confess all soon, and she won't give a damn. Promise you. No, can't come to see you just now. Too busy. All the hoo-ha about the rescue and whatnot has held us up. Back to normal soon. Righto. Just play it along. Thanks for ringing. No, nothing to worry about now. So long, Jim."

Lindsay heard the receiver replaced. She lay there, with the phone still in her hands, waiting till she would hear Euan go outside so she could replace this one without being heard.

Then she realized he was coming upstairs, two at a time. She gave a loud cough, and under cover of it, got the telephone back on its cradle.

She turned on her pillow, pretended to be asleep. Oh, the cough! She gave another little one, let it die away, kept her eyes shut. He came to the door, stood there looking at her, then stole away.

Tears forced themselves from under her closed lids. So much for instinct . . . so much for being sure Euan must be above suspicion, that he could explain all satisfactorily. He'd found a way of

lulling her suspicions . . . had he, indeed!
Euan Hazeldean was in for a big shock
once she got better. How gullible could
women be? And he actually thought
that once they were engaged, she would
approve his actions! Presumably because
she would then share in the proceeds.
If her little sister and brother therefore
got less, it was not supposed to matter
to her!

As she remembered the ghastly,
compensating, terrible yet sweet time
down the mine shaft, a band of pain
gripped her heart, her head. Odd how
mental anguish could be physical, too,
or so it seemed.

By nightime all the pains had fused
together. Lindsay had developed a raging
fever, was bright eyed, complained of a
tightness in her chest, a pain in her side.
The doctor, hastily summoned, diagnosed
pleurisy and ordered the ambulance.
There could be complications, it was
beyond home nursing, and she was
whisked off to Dunstan Hospital in
Clyde. Lindsay didn't care. She didn't
care about anything.

Nothing mattered save that Jock of

Hazeldean was a liar. A liar and a cheat and a thief . . .

★ ★ ★

One thing about being really ill, Lindsay thought, a week later, was that nobody worried you about anything. If you closed your eyes they thought you were asleep. If you didn't want to discuss anything you had only to sigh, to put your hand to your head, and they stopped.

In another week she was on her feet, but was not allowed to go home. They arranged for Jenny to take her to Queenstown. Madeleine and Mrs. Linmuir were running the shop. Mrs. Ford had done all Mrs. Linmuir's baking — a community effort.

"I would like to be home," said Lindsay restlessly.

Euan said gently, "You can't come yet, Lindsay. If my mother were home to look after you it would be all right . . . I did call her, but the whole family has had flu. But the doctor said he didn't want you in the Accommodation House by yourself at first. He said you would be tempted to serve at busy times, and you mustn't for at least another two weeks. So Madeleine offered this bit of service. Let her do it . . . she needs something to do just now."

Lindsay's eyes lifted quickly to his face, found herself unable to read his expression, dropped her glance again. Euan was looking at her in puzzled fashion. He thought, naturally, that he had pulled the wool over her eyes, down there in the mine shaft. Now, of course, he could not understand her listlessness, her lack of response. But you couldn't have a showdown with a man while you were in a public ward, and fortunately, neither could he foist his false caresses on you. A good thing they were not formally engaged.

She wondered what he meant about Madeleine. Her mind wandered around the subject. Did he mean that Madeleine knew there was an understanding between them? She'd said nothing to anyone, but it wasn't to say Euan hadn't. But Madeleine wouldn't break her heart over that . . . she didn't love Euan. Or her mother wouldn't have had to contrive so much. She did love the kind of life Euan led.

She puzzled around the situation between herself and Euan. He must be so deeply in at Rhoslochan that rather than have her find out and expose him, he would marry her. What sort of man would do that? Maybe she had been nearer the mark than she knew when she had called him cold-blooded. Evidently it was more important to keep her quiet about things on the estate than for him to court Madeleine, with all her prospects and future property.

These thoughts mulled around in her brain so she hardly heard what Euan was saying.

"Mrs. Ford will let you have their weekend cottage at Frankton Arm, on Lake Wakatipu. It's quite charming, built to the sun, very gay, with Mexican decor. You'll grow brown and strong there, Lindsay if that fair skin of yours ever does brown. You'll certainly freckle. I told you I liked freckles, didn't I?" He grinned, but got no answering grin back. "You're to laze, walk, bathe, lie in the sun. Jenny will take you in her mother's car. It will be handy for running around. One thing, though, you're not to go on the Skippers' bus."

Lindsay said, "What Skipper? And why a bus, not a boat?"

Euan chuckled. "Mick will enjoy that one! The Skippers' bus, my loved one, is the minibus that does the Skippers' Canyon run. It's breathtaking, but after your fall down the shaft I don't want your nerves subject to any strain."

It took Lindsay all her time not to let her lip curl. This solicitude was such mockery. What a man! Why must she fall for men not worthy to be loved?

He said, in a lower voice, "If you're worrying about what we'll do about the shop when we — when we settle our affairs — it's solved. Alec Linmuir is pretty shrewd, he's got a fair idea of how things are shaping. He said to me last week, 'If ever Lindsay finds she doesn't want to carry on with the tearooms, I'd like the chance of leasing them for Jenny. It will keep her home.' So I said, 'Okay. If ever that happens, we'll let you have an option.'"

Lindsay stirred uneasily, looked out of

311

the window beside her at the dark hills that loomed over the gorge not far away. She said, "Yes. Euan, it's past visiting time, and they do have a rush here before tea."

He got up, nodded goodbye to the other patients, smiled at her from the door, and left.

★ ★ ★

The holiday at Queenstown, nestled under the heights on the shore of the intensely blue lake, was perfect as regards weather, scenery, and Jenny's company. Lindsay tried to respond to it all, to appreciate what was being done for her, and failed.

Outwardly she looked fit. Her skin acquired a faintly apricot glow, the predicted new freckles appeared on the bridge of her nose, she had regained a little weight. But she knew she would have no peace of mind till she got home and had it out with Euan. She would tax him with that telephone conversation, demand to know everything, and that restitution must be made if there were discrepancies.

She must not allow her feelings . . . her former feelings, she hastily amended . . . to stand in the way.

She had one letter from him. No visit. It wasn't even a real love letter.

I would like to write as I long to write, Lindsay, but there are things to be cleared up between us first. Many things. This business of young Lockhart, for instance. But I can't force any major decisions upon you till you're really yourself again. There need be no hurry. But don't stay away too long, will you, Lindsay?

She stared at it incredulously. He was still harping on about Alastair coming out. And taking a lot for granted. Oh, but there was a rude awakening ahead of Jock of Hazeldean!

He was right in one thing. She wasn't going to stay away too long. Too much time had elapsed as it was. She must get things seen to for Neill's sake as well as the twins'. She said to Jenny that she'd like to go home two days early and go as a surprise.

Jenny consented most readily. Lindsay suspected it had something to do with the fact that her brother had a friend staying with him.

They drove home on a glorious early autumn day, with the poplars in the gorges torches of living gold above the green blue of the Clutha. They came to Crannog about five.

Jenny said, "Don't let's go as far as the Accommodation House. It will be the busy time and Madeleine will be flat out. Come up to our place for tea."

Lindsay eagerly clutched at any postponement of the showdown she was going to ask for . . . already her knees felt shaky . . . so she accepted.

Mrs. Linmuir was thrilled to see them, but clucked disapprovingly about their not letting her know. "I've been at the shop all morning. Madeleine always takes the afternoon so I can prepare my dinner. And we were just saying we'd have a grand cleanup of the quarters before you got home, fill the place with flowers and so on. Never mind, we'll just come over tomorrow morning and do it then. We aren't having you overdoing things to start with. But you'd better spend the night with us. Neill's away in Alexandra — some do at the school. Callum and Morag and Bronwen are all at a party and are staying here the night, too. There'll be no one but Jock up at the big house."

Lindsay made up her mind. What better opportunity? "Mrs. Linmuir, you've more than enough with the twins extra, and Douglas's friend. I'd love to be quite on my own tonight. I've things to attend to . . . business mail and so on. Jenny can run me over, and I'll get on with it and quite enjoy being able to do it. No, I shan't be nervous. If I was I would ask Madeleine to stay the night."

Finally Mrs. Linmuir gave in.

Lindsay knew a sense of relief. She'd be able to see Euan quite alone. She would tell Madeleine she didn't want any tea, or that she'd go up and have it at Rhoslochan. Madeleine would be kept at the shop some time yet. And if she were very upset by the time she had finished with Euan, she need not come back till the shop was closed down and she would have the night to get over things without anyone to ask questions. They were surprised to find the Accommodation House closed. They drew up, and saw a notice: Closed.

They looked at each other.

Jenny said, "Well, of course we weren't expected, but Mum thought Madeleine was here. I suppose Jock hasn't — " She stopped.

"You suppose Jock hasn't what?"

She thought Jenny tried to speak casually. "Hasn't taken Madeleine out?" Then she thought of something and was glad to voice it. "I mean this high school concert. Perhaps Madeleine was asked, too, and they've all gone."

Lindsay said coolly, "It's not a concert. I remember now. It's a school dance — not parents or guardians. But I expect Euan *has* taken Madeleine out somewhere."

Jenny spoke without thinking. "And you don't mind?"

Lindsay's voice was crisp. "Why should I?"

Jenny floundered. "No, I suppose not. I — but I — just thought once or twice that he — that you — "

Jenny had never heard Lindsay's voice sound like that before. "You're at the romantic age, Jenny. But not for me . . . with Euan Hazeldean."

Jenny's voice held real disappointment. "But — but it would be so — so *right.*"

"You mean because then the children could be in their very own home?"

"No, I *don't*! I meant that you and Euan are so — "

"We're coguardians of the twins, Jenny, nothing more. I'm sure you're right. He'll be out with Madeleine."

Jenny said, "Well, I think they might have kept the shop open."

"It doesn't matter. Not many calling in at this time of night, perhaps. It's a month since I was here and two weeks since you were Jenny. Business may be tailing off. I'm certainly not going to open up now. They'll have left the back-door key on the nail on the apple tree, I suppose."

"I'll just make sure you get in all right," said Jenny.

They opened up, saw a pile of mail on the kitchen table. Jenny kissed her and went away.

Lindsay made herself a cup of tea, strong. Because she would have to go up to the homestead to see if Euan was there. She began opening the mail. The third letter was from MacWilson's — her monthly cheque for the children, she supposed. Only wasn't it ahead of time?

She opened it. A letter. She began to read, dropped it, and the color left her cheeks. She picked it up again, read on, fascinated, to the end.

Then, this time taking in the meaning less dazedly, she read it through again.

Dear Miss Macrae,

When first I got a communication from Worleson and Pinberry, I contacted Jock and asked him to make a clean breast of things to you. I thought this farce had gone on long enough. He wasn't willing to do anything then — he explained this to me later — and I realized nothing could be done when you were in such a weak state. I trust you are now completely recovered.

However, having known Jock for most of my life I was practically certain he would do himself less than justice when he did tell you, so I decided to tell you myself.

The fact is that the Rhoslochan estate is his, and has been for some years. Alexander Bairdmore got his affairs into a shocking state. He spent lavishly, more than he could afford, while in Europe, for one thing, then between drink, horses and poker he frittered the rest away.

Certain shares in the Rhoslochan estate were always Jock's. His mother did not sell them all out, only the major part. Jock brought it back to prosperity. He worked far too hard, made enough out of his own sheep to keep things going, then finally had to buy Alexander out to save him going bankrupt. It suited Alexander all right. He needed someone to keep a hand on the purse. He did a bit on the farm, whenever he wasn't on the binge, and Jock paid him a generous wage.

Jock kept most of it from Neill. He didn't want to disillusion him too much about his father. He even let the name on the mailbox stay as Bairdmore. Jock planned, if Neill turned out a good farmer, to take him in as a partner when he was old enough to bear the knowledge that his father had frittered away the estate.

Certainly Alexander Bairdmore made the will you say . . . only there was nothing, or practically nothing, to leave. Until he died we had no idea he had got in so steeply. He had surrendered his insurances, there was nothing left. We had known, always had, that he had contracted a marriage that failed, when he was overseas, but nothing more till he told us he had twin children, in the care of his wife's child by a former marriage, one Lindsay Macrae, who we thought was a man — you know all about that.

By that time his mind was wandering, owing to pressure on the brain. He evidently had some hazy idea he could make it all up to the children. Perhaps he had forgotten his money was gone. That's why we were so dismayed when we got your letter — the one you sent Alexander — saying you were coming. We tried to stop you. There was nothing to come for.

Even at that time, Jock said that if you were just a young fellow making your way, he would make you an allowance for the children, out of the estate. But you were on your way. It seems to have worked out very nicely. Jock tells me you've made a grand success of the tea shop.

He's a magnificent chap. He didn't want you to feel penniless in a new country, didn't want the children or you to feel dependent upon his bounty. At first, of course, he was a little wary. But he soon realized you were only anxious for the children.

I think that by now you know Jock so well that matters can be arranged most harmoniously. Please allow him to continue making the allowance to the children. He regards them as family connections, and Jock's a clannish fellow.

You mustn't blame yourself for your suspicions. Jock is — now — only amused at them. He thinks you were very astute. We skated on very thin ice. I've been pushing for some time for the situation to be made clear. I hope you will not find this letter in any way upsetting. Rhoslochan, thanks to Jock's management, is well able to support a whole family.

Do come in and see me next time you're in town, if you wish anything further explained. Perhaps Jock could bring you up to dinner some night. I should very much like you to meet my wife. We could put you both up.

Yours cordially,

James MacWilson

After this second reading Lindsay carefully laid the two-page letter on the kitchen table, meticulously matched the corners, put a vase on top of it.

She stood up and found her knees would support her but were trembling.

The full realization was coming. Rhoslochan was Euan's, the car was Euan's. The Accommodation House had been solely his to give. He hadn't wanted her to know she was penniless in a strange land, stranded, with two children to support . . . even though he had doubts as to her own aspirations and hopes.

The things she had said to him rushed over her . . . the way she questioned him, warned him, taunted him!

But another awareness was breaking like a sunrise now. The remembrance of all that had happened in the unspeakable slime of the old mine shaft. His kisses, his words, the assumption that later on, in a different setting . . . what was it he had promised? Moonlight and roses . . . that he would carry on from there.

Then he did love her, in spite of all she had said to him, in spite of her coldness in the hospital, avoiding his eyes, turning from any tenderness . . . oh, pray heaven he'd just taken it for shyness in a hospital ward. She had not even answered the letter he wrote her at Queenstown. Still, even in that he had assured her he was waiting till they could talk things out.

She remembered what Jenny had said, less than half an hour ago . . . that she and Euan were so *right* for each other. Oh, little Jenny was going to love this!

What an escape from utter folly she had had. By her coldness she might have thrust him into Madeleine's arms. And that would have been tragedy for the three of them. Madeleine might love Euan's way of life, but she certainly didn't love Euan.

Things were unfolding, going right for her. She didn't think any longer Euan was out with Madeleine. He'd be up at the homestead . . . gloriously alone. She could go up to him, tell him she knew . . . now, this very moment. She'd take one of the ponies.

No, she wouldn't. That meant changing into slacks. Slacks and moonlight and roses didn't go together.

Not that it would be moonlight yet. It was nearly sunset, the hour when Rhoslochan was most beautiful of all, when the sun, sinking over the Alps, bathed the whole homestead in amber and mother-of-pearl, staining the little lochan, willow-fringed, iris-edged, with purest rose.

She looked happily down at her blue dress, low-cut, sleeveless, its full skirt swinging. He liked her in blue. She picked up the locket from her breast, said whimsically, "All right, Robert the Bruce, we try again!"

She caught up the letter, ran out of

the house and took the path through the trees.

It would be nice if Euan were having a smoke on the terrace, if he saw her, came to met her, glad she had come home earlier than planned. She came to the garden gate, saw the roses in full bloom, caught their fragrance on the warm, balmy air, smiled, said, kissing her fingertips to them, "See you later . . . in the moonlight!"

No, he wasn't on the terrace. The basket table was there, the newspaper turned down on it, a glass, a pair of scissors. Perhaps he'd gone in to answer the phone. He would turn, see her, hurry up the call.

She went through the French windows. He was not there. She stood in the doorway and called up the stairs. "Euan! Euan . . . it's me!"

No answer. Well, not to feel disappointed. You couldn't have things perfect. He might be just outside, or over at Mick's. Her eye fell on the telephone table, the pad beside it. They always left messages there. There was one there now, in Euan's scrawl: 'Neill, have gone to Dunedin with Madeleine. Won't be back tonight. Will call you tomorrow. Euan.'

She stared at it. Oh, no! She willed it to disappear, to be a figment of her imagination.

She supposed he had taken Madeleine to a show. People here were so crazy about distances. They thought nothing of going over a hundred miles and another hundred back for something special. Lindsay knew a real pang of pure jealousy.

And if he was going to call Neill tomorrow morning it meant he must not be intending to return right after breakfast. Would they stay at Jim MacWilson's? Well, never the time, the place, and the loved one all together, the old adage said. She could almost guarantee that he'd arrive back when she was flat out in the shop!

She almost choked on a sob, then pulled herself up. All that really mattered was that Jock of Hazeldean was *not* a liar, a cheat, a thief. That all their lovely tomorrows were ahead of them.

Anyway, Wynne would know where

and why they had gone. She sat down at the telephone table, had actually got her hand on the receiver when it rang, making her jump.

It was Mrs. Ford. "Oh, gracious, is that you, Lindsay? I thought you weren't getting back for a couple of days yet. Well, it all goes to show that all things happen at once. Nice things as well as nasty. Is Neill there? . . . Oh, of course. I'd forgotten about the school dance. No wonder — I don't know if I'm on my head or my heels. It's so wonderful! Never in my wildest dreams did I think of anything so romantic happening. I don't mind a bit missing out on a white wedding, if my girl has made up her mind at last. Talk about Gretna Green! Just imagine what a lovely piece of family history it will make one day . . . just shows what a mother can do if she's cunning enough. *An elopement!* I just can't believe it. I thought they'd gone out with bustles and crinolines . . . you know, into the saddle and off with you. Pity it had to be a station wagon. Rod's furious, of course, can't see any reason for it at all. Fat lot I care . . . after

327

all, what's a wedding veil and twenty yards of satin compared with knowing your girl didn't make a ghastly mistake and marry the wrong man! What did you say, Lindsay?"

Lindsay felt as if someone had taken hold of her and squeezed the breath out of her body. She couldn't, couldn't go on listening to Mrs. Ford. This was a nightmare, one you didn't wake up from. It was poetic justice for her having entertained those unjust suspicions of Euan . . . only it couldn't be borne, not a moment longer. She said the first thing she could think of.

"Sorry, Fordsy, I've got to go. There's someone at the door, they've been ringing some time. Look, I'll call you later. Yes, yes, it's thrilling. I rejoice with you — "
Oh what a liar you are, Lindsay Macrae
" — but I must go. Goodbye for now."

The receiver crashed out of her nerveless fingers back on to its cradle.

She stood up, staring blankly at the wall, gathered up MacWilson's letter, turned and crossed the room, passed through the French windows, went blindly down the terrace, down the steps, through the fragrant, weedy garden, through the rose arch and down the paddocks to the lochan.

She stumbled as she went, but didn't heed the stones in her way, not stopping till she came to the flat rock she always sat on to dream over the lochan.

Now she flung herself down on it and wept helplessly. Were there any sadder words in the language than 'too late'?

Behind her the sunset pulsed and glowed, the mountains were silver and purple, their peaks like jagged cardboard cutouts against the painted splendor of the sky. The weeping willows swept the rose pink waters with gentle green fingers.

Lindsay felt almost beyond feeling, all emotion wept out of her, a calm after the storm.

Into the stillness a voice spoke behind her, a voice that had the suggestion of a laugh in it.

"Why weep ye by the tide, ladie?
    Why weep ye by the tide?
Young Lockhart comes frae Scotland
        soon,
    And ye shall be his bride!"

There was a silence, then, "With apologies to Sir Walter Scott, Lindsay. Love makes me poetical. Were you weeping because you found me from home, Lindsay, when you came early? Or have you read Jim's letter?"

She couldn't speak. She couldn't turn. Because she must be dreaming. And when she turned around nobody would be there.

Then she said, to the lochan in front of her, in the strangest tone Euan had ever heard from her, "but . . . it can't be you . . . can it, Euan? Because you've eloped with Madeleine."

He gave a great shout of laughter, covered the remaining distance between them, reached her, turned her around, looking down on her with the most quizzical expression.

"Lindsay Macrae, what bee have you got in your bonnet now? Elope with Madeleine . . . me? I'd just as soon elope with one of the station ponies! She's been a playmate, never anything more. She's eloped with her artist — that Duncan Besterman. The one she's been eating her heart out for. At least she hasn't

. . . eloped, I mean. Oh, help, where are we? Look, who told you all this?"

She said slowly, "Mrs. Ford did. She babbled as she always does. But coupled with your note to Neill . . . gone to Dunedin with Madeleine . . . plus Fordsy saying wasn't it romantic, Madeleine had eloped, I naturally thought you had. I — I thought that my cruel suspicions of you plus my cold behavior since the rescue had tipped the scales in Madeleine's favor. That it was all my fault. I had just read Jim MacWilson's letter explaining everything. No, Euan, not yet. Before you . . . before we . . . well, before everything else, let me get it straight. Where is Madeleine?"

His answer was most unexpected. "Back home at Westeringhill. She didn't read the morning paper till latish. She was busy at the tea shop. Then she discovered the report of a car accident on the Kilmog. Two chaps in Dunedin Hospital, one badly injured. He was named as Duncan Besterman. Madeleine lost no time. She charged up here, having shut the shop, told me to get her to Dunedin before Duncan died thinking she was a selfish little beast who wouldn't leave her horses to follow him around the Pacific. Actually, when we got there we found it was the chap in the other car — whose fault it was — who had the broken pelvis. Duncan was merely shaken. We brought him back.

"I hadn't realized the silly wench hadn't rung her mother before we left. It shows how upset Madeleine was — so as soon as she knew he was all right, she rang her mother, and from what you've told me either she or Fordsy were too excited to get it straight. Fordsy thought she was marrying Duncan there and then. Not me, you darling idiot! You know what an addle-pated romantic Fordsy is. Trust her! And of course, coupled with my note, no wonder you thought that. Not that I stopped at Westeringhill to sort things out. Fordsy said you were home. I had called Jim while in Dunedin and found out he'd written you, so I left the Fords welcoming their prospective son-in-law and belted over here."

Lindsay was still struggling with unbelief. "Welcoming? But isn't Fordsy furious it isn't you Madeleine is marrying?"

Euan stared. "But you've known all along she wanted Maddy to marry Duncan, didn't you? That she was terrified Madeleine was going to make the mistake of putting the life she loved before the man she loved, and knowing what a contrary little puss Maddy is, she kept ramming me down her throat. Fordsy said she'd told you. She was pretending Madeleine had cause to be jealous of you — over me. It only amused me. But I thought you knew the real idea."

Lindsay was beginning to smile. "She never does finish a sentence. She told me just about as adequately as she told me about the supposed elopement. That's why I thought — "

She stopped.

Euan said, coming nearer, "That's why you said what you did that night I was kissing you when you were bandaging my finger and you made me hopping mad?"

She nodded, but put up a hand to ward him off. "Wait . . . let's get this straight. I'm ready to grovel, Euan, for thinking what I did about you, for — "

He shook his head. "No matter, Lindsay, this is just wasting time. I could use it better. Oh, well, if you must. You see, by the time you were here a week, I was falling for you . . . hard. I've things to regret, too. I've never forgiven myself for the welcome you got at Momona. I can't bear to think of it.

"By the time we got into town I had realized that although, apparently, you might have come for what you could get out of the estate, at least the children were the responsibility of the estate, and I dared not risk having you refuse help. As you would have done had you realized your stepfather had nothing to leave.

"You see, Lindsay . . . now don't get mad with me, because I realize now it couldn't have been a fair statement of how things really were . . . years ago, when I asked Lex straight out where his money was going, he said he'd married in Scotland, that his wife had married him for his money and refused to come to New Zealand with him, had called it a Godforsaken spot at the ends of the earth, and that she expected him to keep her in style over there . . . and he had. I was bitter about it. I thought that that explained why he had gone to the pack.

"I blame myself now for having accepted that at its face value. I shouldn't have, knowing Lex."

A faint radiance was beginning to dawn on Lindsay's face.

But Euan continued. "And you see it wasn't till last night that I found out about Alastair Lockhart. Alec suddenly mentioned his wife, his boys. I nearly fell flat on my face. I questioned him. Mrs. Alec was there, and fortunately she knew a bit about it. You see, Lindsay, I'd had a letter from Feadan . . . remember? From Mrs. Abernethy. She'd met Mrs. Lockhart, heard her say her son Robin was engaged to a girl who had come out here to see about an inheritance. Not that the engagement was broken off. But Mrs. Linmuir told me last night. That you broke off the engagement because he wouldn't accept the responsibility of the children. That's why I said we had things to discuss. I was sure you loved me, after that hour down the mine shaft, but I had to find out about Robin."

She made a vague gesture as if to dismiss Robin and all he meant. "That doesn't matter. Euan, what you said before . . . do you mean you didn't know? I mean I think you're going to clear up the last doubt in my mind . . . the reason why I thought you the harshest man I'd ever met. I asked you once if you knew why my mother's second marriage had broken up, remember?"

His eyes narrowed. "Why, yes, Lindsay, I do remember. Tell me, in as few words as possible, why it broke up . . . because I'm getting impatient."

"My mother was expecting twins. Some unforeseen kidney complication occurred. She . . . went completely blind, Euan. Lex couldn't take it. Couldn't take being tied to a blind woman for the rest of his days. He fled. It nearly killed my mother, my gay, gallant little mother — the disillusionment. Because she had loved him, Euan. She never told him that she regained her sight after the babies were born. Didn't tell him there was more than one. She accepted an allowance — for one — till they were five and she could go back to teaching again.

"Oh, don't look like that Euan . . . *you didn't know*. We've both hurt each other deeply . . . but in ignorance. We've got the rest of our lives . . . here in the loveliest place in the world . . . to make it up to each other."

Euan's hand had come to his mouth; he bit his knuckle, choked back all he would have said.

He put his hands out and pulled her to her feet. The last rays of the setting sun lit up her face, showed the traces of her weeping. She was outlined there, against the faint pink of the lochan, her blue skirt billowing out. He looked down on her.

Suddenly they were nudged apart. They looked down. Rory, the big golden Labrador, wriggled in between them, lay down across their feet with a satisfied grunt.

"That darned dog!" said Euan. "He's in on everything. All right, old boy. Lie still." His eyes were tender. "No more divided loyalties for him!"

The dark face was very near hers, his hazel green eyes under their overhanging brows ardent.

"Tell me, Lindsay, tell me true
. . . *were* you letting the tears down
fall for Jock o' Hazeldean?"

"Yes, Jock," said Lindsay Macrae.

THE END

NO ROSES IN JUNE
THROUGH ALL THE YEARS
· BACHELORS GALORE
NEW ZEALAND INHERITANCE
REVOLT — AND VIRGINIA

Other titles in the
Ulverscroft Large Print Series:

TO FIGHT THE WILD
Rod Ansell and Rachel Percy

Lost in uncharted Australian bush, Rod Ansell survived by hunting and trapping wild animals, improvising shelter and using all the bushman's skills he knew.

COROMANDEL
Pat Barr

India in the 1830s is a hot, uncomfortable place, where the East India Company still rules. Amelia and her new husband find themselves caught up in the animosities which seethe between the old order and the new.

THE SMALL PARTY
Lillian Beckwith

A frightening journey to safety begins for Ruth and her small party as their island is caught up in the dangers of armed insurrection.

THE WILDERNESS WALK
Sheila Bishop

Stifling unpleasant memories of a misbegotten romance in Cleave with Lord Francis Aubrey, Lavinia goes on holiday there with her sister. The two women are thrust into a romantic intrigue involving none other than Lord Francis.

THE RELUCTANT GUEST
Rosalind Brett

Ann Calvert went to spend a month on a South African farm with Theo Borland and his sister. They both proved to be different from her first idea of them, and there was Storr Peterson — the most disturbing man she had ever met.

ONE ENCHANTED SUMMER
Anne Tedlock Brooks

A tale of mystery and romance and a girl who found both during one enchanted summer.

CLOUD OVER MALVERTON
Nancy Buckingham

Dulcie soon realises that something is seriously wrong at Malverton, and when violence strikes she is horrified to find herself under suspicion of murder.

AFTER THOUGHTS
Max Bygraves

The Cockney entertainer tells stories of his East End childhood, of his RAF days, and his post-war showbusiness successes and friendships with fellow comedians.

MOONLIGHT
AND MARCH ROSES
D. Y. Cameron

Lynn's search to trace a missing girl takes her to Spain, where she meets Clive Hendon. While untangling the situation, she untangles her emotions and decides on her own future.

NURSE ALICE IN LOVE
Theresa Charles

Accepting the post of nurse to little Fernie Sherrod, Alice Everton could not guess at the romance, suspense and danger which lay ahead at the Sherrod's isolated estate.

POIROT INVESTIGATES
Agatha Christie

Two things bind these eleven stories together — the brilliance and uncanny skill of the diminutive Belgian detective, and the stupidity of his Watson-like partner, Captain Hastings.

LET LOOSE THE TIGERS
Josephine Cox

Queenie promised to find the long-lost son of the frail, elderly murderess, Hannah Jason. But her enquiries threatened to unlock the cage where crucial secrets had long been held captive.

THE TWILIGHT MAN
Frank Gruber

Jim Rand lives alone in the California desert awaiting death. Into his hermit existence comes a teenage girl who blows both his past and his brief future wide open.

DOG IN THE DARK
Gerald Hammond

Jim Cunningham breeds and trains gun dogs, and his antagonism towards the devotees of show spaniels earns him many enemies. So when one of them is found murdered, the police are on his doorstep within hours.

THE RED KNIGHT
Geoffrey Moxon

When he finds himself a pawn on the chessboard of international espionage with his family in constant danger, Guy Trent becomes embroiled in moves and countermoves which may mean life or death for Western scientists.

TIGER TIGER
Frank Ryan

A young man involved in drugs is found murdered. This is the first event which will draw Detective Inspector Sandy Woodings into a whirlpool of murder and deceit.

CAROLINE MINUSCULE
Andrew Taylor

Caroline Minuscule, a medieval script, is the first clue to the whereabouts of a cache of diamonds. The search becomes a deadly kind of fairy story in which several murders have an other-worldly quality.

LONG CHAIN OF DEATH
Sarah Wolf

During the Second World War four American teenagers from the same town join the Army together. Forty-two years later, the son of one of the soldiers realises that someone is systematically wiping out the families of the four men.